May

For Stephan

May

Naomi Krüger

SEREN

Seren is the book imprint of
Poetry Wales Press Ltd
57 Nolton Street, Bridgend, Wales, CF31 3AE
www.serenbooks.com
Facebook: facebook.com/SerenBooks
Twitter: @SerenBooks

ISBNs
Paperback – 978-1-78172-428-6
Ebook – 978-1-78172-429-3
Kindle – 978-1-78172-430-9

A CIP record for this title is available from the British Library.

The publisher acknowledges the financial assistance of the Welsh Books
Council.

Printed in Bembo by Bell & Bain Ltd, Scotland.

6:15 am

There was a boy   *a very strange enchanted boy.*   *They say he*
wandered very far   *very far*   *over land and sea.*   *A little shy –*
Go away, I can sing if I want to –
and sad of eye –
Keep singing and they'll go away –
but very wise   *was he –*
Don't look, don't look, don't look –
And then one day   *one magic day he passed my way*   *and*
while we spoke of many things fools and kings   *this he said to*
me   *the greatest thing*   *you'll ever learn*   *is*

just keep singing till he comes

14 January 2000

Afsana

I get off the bus and there's a song in my head. Something from one of the Bollywood films Amina used to tape off the TV late at night. A love scene, probably. I don't remember any words. The sky is streaked with bright pink and peach. It looks unreal behind the buildings. It looks like a backdrop. I'm early. I stand here and look at the lights on in the bedrooms, the shadow of someone behind the glass, the empty smoking shelter. This place has never looked uglier. All the windows are too small and in the wrong places. The bricks are too new. Cheap-looking. Five minutes until the shift starts. I'm not dreading going in, not like in the beginning. I just want to stand here and look at it for a little bit longer. These colours. This sky.

I take the shortcut through the gap in the fence. I can smell burning toast before I even open the staff door. Bags and coats and lockers and voices from the corridor and the smell of the place. It's hard to pin down. In the staff room Alison is putting photos from the Christmas party on to the noticeboard.

'Sana!' she says, 'just the person. Can you sort May out this morning? She's refusing to get dressed. Gill's already tried.'

'Ok.'

'She seems to like you.'

She catches me looking at the pictures.

'Oh God, I look a right mess don't I? I promise you I wasn't as drunk as I look there. You should've come. It was a laugh.'

'Maybe next time.'

'You don't have to drink, you know, if that's what's worrying you.'

'No – it was just – I had something else on that night.'

'I'll let you know when we're next going out. You have to come. I'll order you a shot of lime cordial.'

I laugh. There's no arguing. She's convinced it's a religious thing. But it's not just the alcohol. Ewan would've insisted on tagging along. I couldn't face him being the only partner there, his hand on my arm all night, the introductions and looks. The never-ending questions.

I stand in front of the mirror and smooth the hair down around my face. The plait is messy from the journey but I can't be bothered to re-do it. I could just cut it all off. One snip of the scissors, that's all it would take. The lightness. Amina would say I don't have the bone structure for something so drastic. But I could do it. And if it didn't look good I could always start wearing the hijab again. Ewan would just love that.

Sometimes, bits of the prayers come back to me, and the surahs they drummed into us at mosque after school. *Guide us, oh Lord on the straight path and not the path of those who have gone astray or who have earned thy wrath.* They took the translations away after a while. *Look to the true source, Sana. Have faith in the holy words.* But all the words merged into one, in the air and on paper. Close my eyes and I can hear the music. I can see the black curves, the half-moons and dashes and tiny little diamonds. Speech marks that aren't speech marks. Sixty-six and ninety-nine. The words just wouldn't speak to me. Baba would test us sometimes before bed. We recited together. He never seemed to notice I was always a split second behind Amina.

I knock on the door of May's room and go in. The curtains are still drawn. She sits on the bed in her nightdress, hunched forward. Rubbing her hands together. I sit down next to her. There's a sour smell. Her hair is lank. She doesn't look up but puts her hand on my leg and breathes out as if she's been waiting.

'He's coming,' she says.

'Who?'

'The boy.'

'That's good. I'm going to turn the shower on. I'll make the water nice and warm for you.'

'You have to be careful with the water. Even a little bit. At his age, even a little bit can be dangerous …'

'There's no need to worry about the water, May.'

Time is getting on. She should be in the dining room for breakfast already. She tries to say something as I lift her nightdress over her head.

'What was that?'

'Doctor Foster went to Gloucester.'

I don't know what to say to that so I help her stand up. She leans against me, then steps back and takes a good look.

'What's your name?'

'Afsana.'

'Of course. That's right.'

She touches the end of my plait. 'All this,' she says, 'where did it come from?'

'My hair you mean? The colour?'

She nods.

'My father's side.'

'So much of it.' She pulls on it, again, not hard, but I have to stop myself backing away. Her face is too close. She puts her other hand onto her head, pointing to her hair lying so flat and dull against her scalp.

'Generous,' she says.

'Not really. He kept plenty for himself. He has a long beard like this.' I mime it coming down to my waist. It could be that long by now for all I know. She smiles and I turn her towards the bathroom and walk with her and sit her on the stool while I turn the water on. There's no way to escape the first freezing blast of it because the dial is directly below the showerhead. Stupid design. I think of Baba sitting on the floor with his legs crossed talking to a friend, someone important. I can't remember which house we were in. There were so many. Amina whispered my instructions in the hallway. We peered through the door for a minute then she gave me a push. I tiptoed across the carpet and sat on his knee facing away from the others. He didn't tell me to go. My cheek against his shirt. He smelt of outside places, of paper and mopped floors and money. I pulled the cup of water towards me and dipped my finger in. I carried the drops over quickly and balanced them onto the hairs in his beard. I held my breath. Nobody noticed. His breathing against me. The shake of his chest when he laughed. The water settled there like dew in a spider's web. Amina snorted from behind the door and my hand shot out. The cup tipped over. Baba gasped and jumped up. The knee of his suit trouser was soaked. He pushed me forward.

'Out!' he said, 'out, out, out! Stop pestering me. Go and do something useful!' I ran out to the stairs. Amina was already at the top.

'I can't believe you actually did it,' she said, 'silly, silly Sana. You know you'll be in for it later.'

May is saying something now but I can't hear her for the rush of the water. I help her onto the shower seat and she doesn't protest. The water runs into her eyes and she closes them. She puts her head down and crouches forward so it runs in a stream down her back. Her skin is pale and papery. Red blotches where the water hits it. I turn the dial away from the hot setting. Just a little. A quarter of an inch. There's a loud knock on the door.

'Ok, ok! I'm nearly done here!'

Gloves on. Soap out. May starts to rock back and forth, she's saying something but I can't make it out.

'I know,' I say. 'Let's just get this over with as quickly as we can.'

I can smell lunch cooking while I'm walking May in to have her breakfast. It's enough to turn your stomach. Over-boiled vegetables and gravy. Almost like the roast dinners Mum used to cook before the cancer, before Dadi moved over from Pakistan to look after us and changed everything. 'Indulge me,' Mum would say to Baba as she put the dishes on the table, 'for just this one thing.' She sang while she peeled the vegetables. She dressed up on Sundays. She wore a shalwar kameez and eyeliner that made her eyes look even bluer than normal. It was like she was putting on a costume. As though she was trying to balance out the Englishness of the food. I asked her once why she always cooked it if she knew he didn't like it. She smiled and bent over and whispered in my ear, 'I'll tell you a secret, Sana – but you have to promise never to tell it to anyone else.'

I nodded. She leant in closer until I could feel her lips on my ear lobe, until it tickled and I couldn't bear to wait any longer.

'Roast potatoes are your Baba's absolute favourite.'

'Then why doesn't he say so?'

She laughed. 'Because if we all said what we were really thinking, the world would probably stop spinning.'

I imagined our funny little island on the globe in Baba's study, gliding round out of sight, stuck in darkness forever.

'Did I tell you he has red hair?' May whispers as I pull a chair out for her and spoon some gloopy porridge into a bowl.

'You mean Arthur, May? Your husband?'

'No, not him. The boy.'

'I think you might have mentioned it.'

She has mentioned it thousands of times, but Gill says it

doesn't do any good to let her get worked up. The boy is special. The boy has hair like fire. He's always running. Sometimes she wants to catch him and sometimes she's desperate to let him get away. I hand her a spoon and she holds it up to her face like she's looking for her reflection.

'You'll know him when he comes won't you? You'll bring him to me?' she says.

I stand with the trolley for a minute and watch them all. They doze in the ugly chairs. Everyone angled towards the TV, like it's a jinn that has them hypnotized. Almost visiting time. There's a quiz show on, and when someone opens the door it has to compete with the sound of an advert for double-glazing from the radio in the staff room. *Why not book a free, no-obligation quote from one of our expert advisors today?* Someone grabs my arm. I jump and the cups and saucers on the trolley rattle.

'Albert! You gave me a scare.'

'Did I my love? Did I? I'm very sorry.' He looks at me, pushing his head right back into the chair. I move round to the front of him. Not too close. His eyebrows are wilder than ever. Like he's been trying to make himself look mad.

'What can I get for you?'

'Did I ever tell you about El Alamein?' he says.

There's a blast of music through the doorway. *Where you from you sexy thing?* a phone ringing, something dropped in the kitchen. It's hard to concentrate. I pour him a cup of tea. Three sugars and no milk. I offer him the plate of biscuits but he waves it away and holds onto my sleeve.

'You remind me of one of the desert girls,' he whispers, 'the girls with the dark hair. In the day they covered it up, but at night...' He winks.

Gill is watching me from the doorway, tapping her watch. I move the trolley on, steering wide around Albert's chair. He recites the tail end of a poem at me as I leave. The same one as usual. *De-dum, de-dum, de-dum, de-dum. I think it's a shame and a sin, for a lion to go and eat Albert, and after we've paid to come in.*

I think of lions and deserts and women with chiffony veils wafting about beckoning men into caves. I'm sweating now. The heat always up too high when the relatives come. I try to smell myself, without anyone noticing, to check for dark patches under the arms of my uniform. There's no time to do anything about it.

I pour May's tea but she doesn't want to talk. She's watching a bird at the window. The first time I've seen one using the feeder Alison put up. It's perching there on the clear plastic, attached to the window with transparent suction cups. Almost like it's trying to get in. A brown bird pecking away. I wish I knew its name.

'Five for silver, six for gold,' she says, then shakes her head as if to make the rest of the words come loose, 'no. That's not right at all.'

And then the visitors are signing in at the reception desk. May's daughter and someone else with her. A teenager. Maybe older. I've never seen him here before. He's too thin. Cheekbones like blades under his skin. Hair hidden under a black hat. Almost. Red hair. *Hair like fire.* And I say it without thinking because it seems so obvious.

'He's here, May. The boy. He's come to see you.'

She sits up and squints towards reception as he gets nearer. Her face so full of hope. I smile at him but he looks away. He has his hands in his pockets. And then May is banging her hand down on the armrest. The teacups rattling again.

'That's not him at all,' she says. 'He was never that big. They're always lying to me. They want to pretend he's not lost.'

'Calm down, Mum,' the daughter says. And the boy has his arms folded now, backing into the corner like he wants to disappear. But May is only getting more unsettled, her voice getting louder and louder. She puts her hands over her ears and starts singing again.

In the flat I watch Ewan shove a forkful of pasta into his mouth. It's the kind of food Mum used to make on weeknights when Baba was out checking his houses, collecting deposit money from the endless stream of new tenants. The TV is on. National news. Some village down south that's been flooded. A man canoeing past a Post Office. Ewan eats with his mouth slightly open, blowing air through the food to cool it down, eventually taking a sip of drink and swallowing it all down together.

'Hot,' he says, 'you not eating?'

'Yeah, I'm just tired.'

'Good news today.'

'Oh?'

'Phil handed in his notice.'

'Oh?'

'You know, Mr Mellor – head of Humanities?'

'I remember.'

'So – they're hoping to fill his place internally. Sally gave me the nod. Unofficially of course, but if I get it –'

'That's great, Ewan.'

'If I get it then it might be time to make some decisions.'

'Decisions?'

'About your work. You hate it, and I'll be earning more,' he pauses and puts his fork down, 'you could get a part time job in town and... you know...'

'What?'

He just looks at me.

'Oh. Right.' *Getting married. Starting a family.* It all sounds so delicate. Like nudging a domino and watching as the whole snaking line of them starts to fall down. He's still looking at me. He thinks it'll mend everything and make it right. Nothing can do that. There's no way to go back. I shake my head to clear it. What am I supposed to say? I can't stop thinking about May and the boy I should never have got her hopes up like that. The terrible look on his face.

'I don't hate my job. Why would you assume that I hate it?'

'Sana. Were you listening to what I just said? Are you even going to bother to give me an answer?'

I shrug. 'It's just – it's not really something I can get my head round at the moment.'

He starts eating again. Turns the volume up on the TV. I

look around at this little room and Ewan's books and piles of marking and the peeling wallpaper in the corner. So bland and bare compared to home. However often we moved, the first thing Mum did was hang the red curtains, roll out the patterned rugs.

'Ewan,' I say, 'do we have a dictionary somewhere? There was this word Gill mentioned in the staff meeting—'

'Are you serious?' he spits out the words, 'is this your way of changing the subject? Unbelievable, Sana. You're so fucking oblivious sometimes.'

The word hits me like a sting. I'm not used to it, even now.

'I'm sorry. I just wanted —'

'You're trying to put it off – like you put everything off. You're more interested in them – they're already dead. I'm talking about life, about making a family.'

I look at him and he stares back, waiting for something, demanding something. I have nothing to give. He scrapes the last of the pasta from the bowl. Sucks it off the fork and puts the empty dish onto the coffee table. I should say something. Too late now. I wait for him to leave, to go into the bedroom. He gets up and walks out – making a point of not slamming the door.

This is the kind of moment I never imagined when I sat in Geography running my fingers across the graffiti on the desk and watching Ewan write on the whiteboard. I liked his blue tie the best and he was wearing it that day. More formal than the other teachers. Still new. His shirt was always tucked into his trousers. He showed us a video about river courses and erosion. The other girls used to give him a hard time. Stupid answers, messing with Blu Tack and paperclips, dropping pencil cases onto the floor in unison at pre-arranged times. I felt sorry for him. I watched the images from above, the camera panning across flat green fields, the river getting wider, snaking around, looping back on itself. He paused the programme. The screen flickering black and white.

'Can anyone tell me what these bends are called?'

I liked landscapes. I liked maps and contours and plans. Mum caught me in Baba's office once. She let me sit in the swivel chair. She pulled the globe across the desk to show me where he came from. Rawalpindi. She traced a curve from Pakistan, across the sea making the sound of a plane flying. She landed it, her finger plunging right into the English Channel. *Splash!* she said, and then *brrrrrrr*. She pretended to shiver. I laughed and laughed until I couldn't breathe.

'Anyone?' Ewan said.

I put my hand up. The diagrams from the textbook were easy to remember.

'Yes, Afsana?'

'Meanders.'

'Good.' He rubbed out the writing that was on the board and drew a snake-curved river with a blue pen. I looked down at my exercise book. I hadn't written all of the notes from the board. Not even close. I'd have to copy off Freya again, if she'd let me.

'And at this stage the river erodes *laterally*,' he looked at us, at me or was I imagining it? 'Outwards, left and right, the neck of the meander gets narrower and narrower until the two sides join up and the water continues on by the quickest route.' He rubbed out the end of the bend.

'Does anyone know the name for the horse-shoe shaped bit that gets left behind?'

I put my hand up again. I didn't care what they thought of me. Someone whistled from the back of the class. A screwed-up piece of paper flew past my ear.

'Anyone?' he said, 'no? Alright then, Afsana again.' But he was smiling at me when he said it.

'An oxbow lake, sir.'

'Yes. Well done. Amy and Khadijah – am I keeping you awake? No? Let's watch the next section then shall we?'

He asked me to stay behind at the end of class. All the girls laughing and whispering on their way out. Freya put two fingers up behind his head. He shut the door.

He pulled a red folder out. My coursework, the first piece I'd handed in since term started.

'I wanted a word about this. I haven't given any marks out yet so this is between you and me, ok?'

I nodded.

'A *D*, Sana.' He sounded outraged. 'Some of the diagrams are promising but the written work is far below the standard I would expect. You're one of my best students, bright, artic-ulate… this isn't good enough.'

He was waiting for me to speak. I shrugged. I opened my

mouth and took a breath and the air caught in my throat. I put my hand on the desk and looked down at his board markers in their plastic case. He'd opened the folder and the paper was covered in red pen scrawls. I wanted to shove it back in out of sight.

'Nothing to say, Sana?'

'I spent a week on it, sir. I swear. It's the best I could do.'

He sighed. 'I believe you. Don't cry, ok?' He passed me a tissue. 'What about your other subjects?'

I shrugged.

'Do you get any special support?'

I shook my head and thought of Baba coming home from a parents' evening years before. He took me by the shoulders. 'Look to Amina,' he said. 'Take her as your example. Things are more difficult for you. All the more reason to put the hours in. Work hard and we won't need their tests Insha' Allah.'

'Would you like me to look into it?' Ewan said.

'No.'

He was looking at me so strangely then, like he could tell what I was thinking. Close up, his eyes were green, not blue like I'd thought.

'What's wrong, Sana? You can tell me.'

'I'm still new here. We move a lot. It's difficult.'

'Well I know what that feels like.' He was smiling at me like it was him that needed the sympathy, like we had things in common. He put his hand over my hand. I looked down at the desk. The weight of his fingers.

'You'd better go for lunch,' he said.

The newsreader is wearing too much makeup. It makes her look old. Her hair is as stiff as a helmet. She re-caps the main stories. I'll feel bad later. I'll have to make it up to him. I'll tell him I know I'm selfish. I'll tell him I'm trying to change. Push the bowl away and think about May. I can't help it. The images come whether I want them to or not, driving out the pictures of water rushing through shop doorways and people – ordinary people – climbing onto the roofs to get away. Her obsession with the boy starting again. Getting worse because of my stupidity. The enchanted boy. The boy who runs into the trees. He came to the back door once, she said, with nothing on. Not a stitch. And there was frost on the ground. His little toes must have been turning to ice. He was jumping up and down on the spot. Wouldn't even stay still long enough for them to wrap him in a blanket.

But there's nothing at all about him in her memory book. No photos, no records. Only a daughter and never any siblings of her own. Then again, if Dadi ever ended up in a place like that I might not be in her memory book either. It would be easier that way. Better not to exist than to be such a disappointment.

The sound of Ewan moving around next door. I tiptoe to the bookcase and crouch down to look in the bottom shelf. The Concise Oxford Dictionary. Baba had one too, a different edition and not so concise. He kept it high in his office so we had to ask him to get it down when we needed it for homework. I pray the word is spelt how it sounds. Gill mentioned it so casually, as though it was a normal part of conversation.

There's new research, she said, *that suggests that sometimes the best way to keep them happy is just to play along.* The pages are thin like scripture. The words so tiny they move and blend. I run my finger down the list and find it between *confab* and *confect.* *Confabulate.* Con. Fab. U. Late. *Imaginary experiences as compensation for memory loss.* Maybe Ewan's right. I'm just wasting my time on things that don't matter. The boy's not coming. It's all fantasy. Most likely he never existed at all.

7:58 am

       but I remember   the boy   He
runs into the trees. He doesn't have   words
           not ones he speaks   out   in the open.
Mum says he's not ours to be worrying about. We have prob-
lems enough and
      I have to pour the tea   and

      there aren't any trees here, not even behind the win-
dows, not for miles and miles.

Oh! Now is it? There's no need to – I can do it!

Don't take them off thank you
very much for your Cadbury's
Roses, thank you very much, thank
you very, very, very, very, very,
very, very, very much.

The water!
      He stepped in a puddle right up to his middle and
never

and never–

Do you have to?   Too hot, too hot, too hot

cheap soap, white tiles

This is not a hospital

there are no trees   this could be

anywhere   and

3 October 1997

Karen

The bedside clock is ticking. Already five past seven. The toilet flushes and I hear her shuffling back across the landing. I can't leave it like this. Mum's bed so crowded with stuff I don't even know where to start. The girls from college will already be ordering drinks and garlic mushrooms, letting the waiter remove the extra setting. They'll wonder where I've got to for all of five minutes and then carry on regardless. I start lifting piles of clothes and tipping them straight into the washing basket. It's like she hasn't put a load on for weeks. Overdue library books, talcum powder, unopened charity letters and Alex's latest school photo un-mounted and already creased at the corners. I feel the dread seeping in. There's no way I'm going to make it now.

The room smells stale. Worse than mine did the time she unearthed the mouldy lunchbox from under my bed at the end of the summer holidays. She stands in the doorway and I can't even look at her. I look at a photo of Dad on the dressing table instead. It's hard to see him through the dust.

'He'd be ashamed,' I say, 'if he could see you.'

She narrows her eyes. 'You've got no right to move my things.'

'You shouldn't have let it get this bad,' I say, sorting the post into a pile and balancing it on the windowsill, 'it's not healthy. And where on earth have you been sleeping?'

She moves towards me and snatches the photo off the bed.

'Careful!' I say, 'it's creased enough as it is.'

She holds it to her chest, facing outwards so that I can see the bottom of Alex's chin through her fingers.

'You've got no right to interfere with my life,' she says, 'not when you've made such a fine mess of your own.'

If I'd dropped Alex off at the door like usual, I'd be none the wiser. If I hadn't popped in to leave the Avon catalogue, and seen the mess in the hall, I'd be at the restaurant now on my third Bellini. I lean on the bannister, close my eyes and focus on my breathing. Sniff my fingertips. It's still there – bergamot, geranium and clary sage. An anti-stress blend. For a minute it drives everything out. The murmur of the TV from downstairs. I don't think about the wasted French manicure, don't notice the state of the carpet. I open her bedroom door as quietly as I can. She's asleep, or pretending to be, curled up on her side facing away from me towards the window.

When I go downstairs Alex is sprawled across the full length of the sofa. He's watching a nature programme. Something about rainforests. A parrot moving its arse back and forth in an attempt to attract a mate.

'Can you turn it down for a minute?' I say.

He doesn't move.

'Alex!'

'What?'

'Turn it down!'

He sits up and passes me the remote. I put it on mute and balance on the arm of the chair next to him. He angles himself away, pretending to be really interested in the fringe on the footstool.

'Why didn't you tell me?' I say. He doesn't move. I want to shake him but I sit on my hands and try to be patient.

'Answer me, Alex.'

'Tell you what?'

'How bad things are with your Nan.'

'I did.'

'No, you didn't.'

'I told you I didn't want to come here anymore.'

'You said you were old enough to stay in on your own. You didn't say anything about this.'

He rolls his eyes.

'What?'

'You never listen,' he says.

His voice is all wobbly. He's embarrassed and when I try to put my arms around him he pushes me away. How could I have missed so many signs? How could I not have seen that something was wrong?

He covers the side of his face with his hand. All elbows and knees. I should leave him alone, I know I should. But I have to explain.

'We'll sort it,' I say, 'we'll make sure she's alright.'

He shrugs.

'No, really,' I say, 'I haven't been around a lot lately and you've been here too much and it must've been hard. But I thought you'd take care of each other. You always liked coming here. And it's only a couple more months until I'm qualified. Things will be different. I can earn extra. Maybe even stop working at the shop and start my own business.'

'Great. Stinking the house out and massaging strangers in the living room.'

'Alex!'

'Well, it's true isn't it?'

'It's aromatherapy. It's about healing and relaxation. And the money will pay for driving lessons, university.'

'I'm thirteen.'

'You won't be thirteen forever.'

He looks at me. His eyes are almost blue tonight. Always changing. He's too thin no matter what I feed him. Skinny and hunched as though he's constantly expecting the world to kick him in the guts. And his hair. So bright even when it's flattened and moulded to his head. He'd still be wearing his hat now if I hadn't made him take it off. I look for traces of Ian in his face. I watch out for little signs but I never really see it. It's been so long. And with him everything was on the surface. The way he clenched his jaw when he was angry, the muscle in his eyebrow that used to twitch just before he lost control. I see Ian in faces of the lads who hang out next to the Spar shop round the corner, rummaging around in their trackie bottoms and hoiking spit onto the kerb. Their pasty shaved heads, and all that macho energy. But not here. I look at Alex and it's like he never existed.

'It's not always this bad,' he says and his voice is calmer, 'sometimes it's ok. I think she just really misses Granddad.'

I can't talk for a minute. The photos on the mantelpiece. The one of me from high school with my hair the colour of tea sludge. Parted down the middle. Layered and flicked, hanging on either side of my face like a bloody cocker spaniel. I wish I could go back to that moment. Make better fashion choices, undo all the mess. But then I wouldn't have him.

'It's ok,' I say, 'we'll sort something out. But first we need to eat.'

'There's nothing in. I've already looked.'

I reach down for my bag and hand him my purse. 'Go on,' I say, 'take a fiver out and nip across to the chippy.'

By the time he gets back my stomach's started to eat itself. The smell of vinegar from the flimsy plastic bag. Everything's such a mess. I root through the drawer for forks. Elastic bands and half-burnt birthday candles. A bereavement card bent and smeared with grease, resting on top of the wooden spoons. And something else. Poking out from underneath the plastic cutlery tray. The corner of a photograph. I have to lift everything up to get it out.

'Alex! Come and look at this!'

'What?' he says, coming into the kitchen.

I hand him the photo and balance the sweaty bag of food on top of the plates. 'Bring it with you. We'll eat on our knees.'

'It's her dad,' he says once we're settled.

I put my fork down for a minute and grab the photo back.

Black and white, crumpled up and speckled with age. The man is standing outside a Post Office holding his police helmet. The uniform looks like something from a comedy sketch. He's tall and lanky. He looks too fragile to hold a truncheon, let alone use one. My Grandfather. I've never seen him before in my life.

'Bloody hell he looks just like you.' I look up at Alex and back to the photo. 'When did she show you this?'

He shrugs. 'I dunno. Not that long ago. She wanted me to know who I had to thank for the hair.'

'I thought that came from the other side.'

'No. Granddad's was auburn. That's different. It's almost normal.'

I laugh. I reach out to touch his head. He leans back into the sofa, away from me.

I didn't think there were any photos. All she ever said was that he died in the war. And Dad never mentioned anything about him. Only her Mum. *Be thankful she kicked the bucket before you came along*, he whispered once under his breath, *between you and me she was a right piece of work*.

'What's Ned short for?' Alex says, out of the blue.

'What?'

'Ned. The name.'

'Edward, I think. Or Edgar. Something like that.'

He points at the photo. 'But he was called William.'

'Yes.'

'Who's Ned then?'

29

'No idea. Why d'you ask?'

He shrugs. 'No reason, really.'

But his cheeks are going pink. And his face. It's the look he used to have when I caught him hiding cabbage under his mashed potato or stashing conkers in his sock drawer.

'Alex.'

'It's nothing. Just sometimes she calls me Ned by accident,' he says.

I don't know what to say. I sniff my fingers again but the smell is wearing off.

'Sorry, can't help you with that one, buddy.'

I turn the sound up on the TV and he watches monkeys swinging through the rainforest canopy. We pretend it's like any other Friday night. But the photo is there in the corner of my eye. My grandfather, who looks too weak to go to war, to carry stretchers on the battle field, to give commands and solve crimes and make any kind of name for himself. This photo that no one ever showed me. And Ned, whoever he is. It bothers me, this mystery name. Something about it gives me the creeps. There's a noise like falling ash in the chimney. The sound of someone running up the stairs in the house next door.

'Maybe we should take her home with us for a few days, just till she's feeling better,' I say, just thinking out loud.

Alex snorts. 'Good luck with that,' he says, 'she'd never come.'

He's right. She's never liked staying in other people's houses. Being away from her own routine.

'We'll just have to stay here then. I can call in sick tomorrow. Drive home and pick up a few things.'

He shrugs.

'You can help me clean, get things back in a decent state.'

'Whatever.'

We sit on the sofa with our arms almost touching, just watching whatever happens to be on. The leftover chips going cold on the coffee table. Lights flashing through the net curtains every time a car goes past. I want to put my arm round Alex's shoulder, to pull him into me. But there's no point. He'd only move further away. For the time being this – right here – is the closest I'm likely to get.

The day after he was born Mum came to visit me in the hospital. She held him and held him and wouldn't stop looking.

'Oh Karen!' she said, 'he's beautiful. There's just something about little boys isn't there? He's an absolute little love.'

It should've made me happy, her being so besotted. I should've been grateful. All the time they spent together. The country walks, Saturday sleepovers, church on a Sunday, picking him up and making polite conversation over roast beef and Yorkshire pudding. He used to tell me he wanted to move in. If I close my eyes it's like everything is tipping over. The whole world turning upside down.

The fine mess I've made of my life.

And the girls in town will be sipping coffee and sharing a tiramisu. They'll be walking down Church Street, laughing, tripping over their own feet, just seeing where the night will take them. I can't get it out of my mind. That moment. Alex in the hospital. The other babies crying. The smell of disinfectant and the ache and shock of it all. And Mum. The way she looked at him. Like nobody else really existed. Like someone had finally given her the thing she'd always really wanted.

8:25 am

He could be anywhere. *They say he wandered very far   very far   over land and sea.*

They make me spill the milk.
              This spoon disappears when it
              shouldn't.   They hide things to make me
confused.

Sometimes he comes to the backdoor and I give him warm
milk. He never dresses for the
              weather. Gulping the milk before Mum sees. He
jumps up and
              down
gives me things. Then they take them away,
                           the leaf, the feather, a bird's egg
       like a message

I tell him to be careful and he knows
                     because speaking isn't –
there are other ways

And bad people are   people who don't listen and

don't want to.

      Some of these people are beyond   decency

        You could be upside down   inside

out before they'd notice   you could be dancing at the

other end of the   ballroom and not one of them would

    put up with it. Lukewarm milk. This place.

        Hot enough to curdle butter.

29 July 1978

Arthur

A perfect summer's evening. Step out of the pub and there's hardly any change in the temperature. The smell of cut grass and spilt beer. I close my eyes and breathe it in. Everything feels like a blessing. The sun going down behind the row of shops, bathing the pub bins in the last light. A quick whiff of warm rotting food and chip fat. May'll be busy at home – ironing short-sleeved shirts for the holiday and cleaning out the cool-box. She'll have everything sorted. There's no point rushing back.

The door opens again. The lads stumble down the steps to a blast of 'Rivers of Babylon'. Billy tries to do a bit of dancing. The daft bugger. He trips and rams his shoulder into my chest.

'Watch it, mate.'

'There you are, Arthur!' he says, 'the big man, the king of Her Majesty's fine postal service.' So close I can see the acne on his cheeks, the fillings in his bottom teeth.

'Alright, son,' Jim is coming down the steps behind him, draping his jacket over one arm. He puts a hand on Billy's back. 'Time for home.'

'Eh? No, Dad! The night is young – right Arthur?'

'I told you you shouldn't've let him have the last one.'

Jim shrugs, 'it's not every day you turn twenty one.'

'Bollocks to this!' Billy says, 'I'm off into town.' A bus is coming down the road, stopping with a hiss at the traffic lights. 'Lend me some money will yer?'

'Not this time. More than my life's worth. Yer Mum's waiting at home. Come on.' Jim tries to pull him by the arm but he hangs on to me like a kid, like I'm Gandhi or Jesus. I push him away – only gently. He never did have much of a clue about personal space.

'I'm just saying, right, I'm just saying… you're a bloody legend. No word of a lie.'

Jim shakes his head. 'Ok son, let's go before you propose shall we?'

'I'm just saying… the night is young.'

'Some of us 'ave got work in the morning.' Jim helps him down the kerb and out of the path of oncoming traffic. 'Enjoy yerself, you jammy bastard. Not too much gambling mind,' he shouts, 'and whatever you do, leave those classy Welsh birds alone.'

I wave him away, watch him drag Billy round the corner next to the bookies.

I should be going straight home as well, but the night *is* young and after a week of diagonal rain, posting disintegrating envelopes through the doors of the great and good it seems a bloody shame to waste an evening like this. So I walk in the other direction. Past the butcher's, the baker's, the café on the bridge that'll be serving bacon butties in the morning – right about the time we'll be driving over the River Dee.

I walk across the road into the park. A Willy Nelson track I can't quite shake. *She loves him in spite of his ways that she don't understand.* Fast picking guitars. Harmonica used as another kind of percussion. Walking to the beat down the avenue of limes. I can't believe how empty it is. The patterns of sun and shadow like my own special lighting. Sing it under my breath even though I can never quite get his accent. Throw my jacket over one shoulder and strut on the gravel like a catwalk model or a cocky American cop. No bloody excuse for it, except I'm a little bit pissed and there's no one around to tell me to stop being such a tit.

Everything feels like enough. The week's holiday stretching ahead. And no getting up for church on the Sunday. No arse-numbing sermon to dream through. *Then sings my soul.* Worshipping at the shrine of the full English breakfast before braving the jellyfish in Llandudno Bay. Blowing up the dinghy with the foot pump – taking Karen out as deep as she dares and then a bit further. Pretending I can't hear May shouting at us to be careful. Squinting back at the shore and taking it in. The people turning pink. The Great Orme. All those grand bed and breakfasts, painted in deck-chair colours, facing out to sea.

Somewhere in the distance there are girls screaming. Kids in the field throwing sticks and swearing at each other. The shouts of teenage boys. I stop and lean against the mulberry tree. The sound of the stream trickling. On Llandudno pier you can see the waves frothing in the gaps between the wooden slats.

Karen used to be scared looking down, as though she'd be sucked through by the sheer force of the water. Once I picked her up and pretended I was going to chuck her over the side and she screamed and May slapped me on the arm and told me to stop tormenting her. That same year I let go of her hand in the arcade and she was lost for five, ten, fifteen minutes, hiding behind a fruit machine, finally popping out and shouting 'Boo!' – thrilled by the look on our faces. May called me a bloody careless idiot, and I told her I am, I know I am, I always bloody have been.

That song in my head again. Over and over. *Through the teardrops and laughter they'll pass through this life hand in hand.* The sun in my eyes and May at home getting everything sorted so I don't need to worry, so I can just climb into bed and drift off without a care in the world. The sky is shifting. All the blood rushing to my head. I steady myself on a bench then sit down and shade my eyes. The rose garden could do with some care and attention. Those kids again, getting nearer, coming from the path by the duck pond. They stop a few yards away. Three lads in nothing but football shorts, shaking their wet heads like dogs swimming after ducks in the canal.

'Come on then!' The one who shouts it is the cockiest. Taller than the others, tanned and well built, like he's been lifting weights in his bedroom. His head doesn't quite match his body.

'Get your tits out!'

His mates laugh, but they're nervous, not sure whether to

join in, not sure how far to push it. They look around, squinting into the sun. The girls come round the corner, in their tight jeans that flap at the bottom, T-shirts with big stiff collars.

'Piss off, Dickson,' one of them says but she doesn't sound angry. 'If you think you're such a man meet us round the cricket hut in five minutes.'

'Oh yeah?' he says and his sidekicks giggle like children, 'oh yeah?'

'Not so talkative now are you?'

'See you in five, hot stuff.'

I watch them walk off across the grass, practising their not-scared-of-nothing swagger, grinning like idiots. I could've taken Billy on into town. I'm still young. I'm young enough.

The girls are still by the pond, in an excited huddle. I look at them properly for the first time. Karen's there. I sit up. She is. Has she been there all the time, hiding behind the others, out of sight? Press myself back into the hedge. Bloody hell. Karen. I should go straight over there and drag her home. I should do something – not just sit here a little bit pissed like the useless article I am. Too young to be out at this time, surely. Nearly fifteen. Next to the others she looks small, but not as small as I remember from seeing her yesterday at teatime. Is it possible she's grown since then? They're talking, arguing. I lean forward, try to concentrate. She's shrugging at them, looking fed up, staring down into the mud.

'Come on,' one of them says, 'you don't have to do nothin'.'

The other girl grabs her arm and pulls her towards the grass.

'Don't be so shit-scared all the time, Kaz.'

And she's going with them across the grass and I'm just sitting and watching and letting it happen.

I should never have had that third pint. I can't move, can't think what to do. What's May playing at letting Karen stay out till all hours? At home ironing shirts and wiping down the table when her daughter's out here, up to all sorts. I stand up, hold onto the arm of the bench, watch her legging it away from the others, heading towards the main path. They yell at her. They're on their way to the pavilion. She's going home. The relief. I want to shout after her, to run and catch up and hold her hand across the road.

At home I go to undo my laces and lose balance. Steady myself on the shoe rack and force the buggers off, kicking them to the back of the porch next to Karen's purple trainers with the stupid stacked heels. My toes throbbing, socks drenched with sweat, stinking to high heaven.

'Where've you been so long?' May says.

'Out.'

'Care to elaborate?'

'No, I don't care to elab…elaber…. I don't care to – no.'

'Please yourself.'

She goes back to the ironing in front of the TV, some sort of police drama – a car chase through empty docklands.

'Where's Karen?'

'Upstairs packing.'

'Where was she earlier?'

She looks at me. 'Youth group. At the church hall. Why?'

I shrug.

'Something you're not telling me, Arthur?'

'Can't a man just ask about the welfare of his offspring now and then?'

The iron hisses. She sits it upright and swops the pair of pants across to the other leg. 'I thought you were a happy drunk.'

'I'm not drunk.'

She raises an eyebrow.

'Bloody hell, woman. What is this? An interrogation?'

I go back out into the hallway. I'd kick something if my feet weren't already throbbing. I lean on the bannister, torn between going upstairs and leaving the house.

'There's a little bit of trifle that needs eating in the kitchen,' she says, cool as anything, 'if you fancy it.'

Of course I stay. There's nowhere else. I sit at the kitchen table and eat with a giant spoon straight out the serving bowl.

'That's disgusting,' Karen says. She squeezes past to get to the fridge, 'and there's no orange juice.'

'Oranges don't grow on trees, you know.'

She gives me a look, a don't-think-for-one-minute-you're-even-remotely-funny kind of look.

'There's nothing to eat.'

'We're using everything up before the holiday.'

'Great. Then I'll just starve shall I?'

'Have some trifle.'

'Blancmange makes me want to puke.'

'Mmmmmmm.' I suck a great lump of it off the spoon.

'You repel me.' She slams the fridge door, stalks out and runs straight up the stairs. Grace of an elephant and the TV blaring and the ketchup clanking against an almost-empty bottle of milk.

'Forecast's rain!' May shouts from the other room.

But the forecasts aren't always right. A couple of years back they'd said it'd be wet all week and they'd been wrong. It'd held off right until the last day of the holiday. Waiting in a chip shop in Bangor for a lightly battered fish. Perched on the brown-tiled window seat when the heavens opened. Rain dripping down the glass. Enough to make you feel right at home. A group of lads came in and ordered in Welsh. They looked me up and down. I didn't imagine it, whatever May said. Laughing too loud. All the harsh words they knew we couldn't understand.

'Did you see that?'

May was reading the notice board. 'What?'

'The way they looked at me.'

'Who?'

'Them!'

She looked up. They were waiting at the counter pushing each other and laughing. Dressed in their scruffs with razored heads and sweatshirts covered in white paint. No more than nineteen.

'Stop being so paranoid.'

'How long does it take to cook a bloody fish?' I folded my

arms, crossed my legs and uncrossed them again. I felt like an idiot, suddenly, in the pressed chinos and short-sleeved shirt. Middle-aged and stuck in my ways and past it. Karen was in her own little world, doodling on the back of a leaflet with a biro. The lads were paying then and walking to the door bringing the smell of vinegar and turps and curry sauce that made me even hungrier than I already was. I could've sworn one of them winked at me on the way out. If I'd said anything about it to May she would've looked at me like I was losing it. They said something in Welsh – and it could've been anything really – like May said, they could've been talking about the weather. But I made my own translation and it stuck in my head as though it was a verifiable fact: *stupid English twat.*

And maybe this year Karen will tell me where to stick the dinghy and complain about the jellyfish and roll her eyes and ask if she can stay in the car while I buy the chips so she doesn't have to be seen with us. It doesn't take much to embarrass her these days. I only have to breathe.

When I get into bed there's music coming from Karen's room. I can't make it out. The tune doesn't seem to match the beat May puts piles of folded clothes into the suitcases.

'She's going to wake up the neighbours,' she says. 'Just what we need. Betty banging on the wall with her walking stick.'

She looks at me, pauses then stuffs a pair of underkecks into the inside mesh pocket. This is my cue to do something. But I'm knackered. Everything's a blur. Tongue still tingling with toothpaste. And the music isn't that loud, really. I could close my eyes and start to drift and maybe I do because before I know it she's out on the landing herself, knocking louder than the beat of the song. The door opens and then I know the song because it's the same one from the pub, the same one that's playing everywhere. *Now how shall we sing the Lord's song in a strange land?* May says something in that tone she has and Karen's shouting. The door slams. Then silence.

'Thanks so much for your help,' she says, huffing back into the room. She carries on balling up pairs of socks and stuffing them into any available corner.

I want to ask her how many miles she's walked today. I want to say *why can't you be more gentle with her? Why does every little thing have to be a full-blown drama?* I want to tell her that sometimes, when they argue, she reminds me, just a little bit, of her mother.

'You're tired,' I say, 'come to bed.'

She mutters something as she zips up the cases, switches off the lamp and climbs in. We settle into the usual tangle. Her skin leaking heat, toenails scratching my shin.

'Ow.'

'Sorry.'

I feel her relax against me. Her hair still stiff with hairspray.

She sighs. 'That test tube baby was born the other day,' she says.

'What?'

'The first one – in Oldham. They implanted it straight into her womb.'

'Bloody hell.'

'Can you imagine?'

I can't. I think of the baby bird I saw in spring. Fallen from the nest. The raw pinkness of it — lying there on the path neatly, inside the lines of a perfect paving slab in a pristine dead-end cul-de-sac. And then the other thing, the shrunken boy. The little one we never talk about.

'Is it normal?'

'What?'

'The baby.'

'Yes. A girl. They called her Louise.'

May's breathing starts to change. I try to listen, to hear any sign of Karen awake across the landing. Nothing. It'll be a long drive tomorrow. The journey is always the best bit. All the things you're going to do. Packing the car with so much stuff you can't see out the rear window. Passing round the Murray Mints. The anticipation. Karen'll be sulking in the morning. But I've still got the magic touch. I'm not past it yet. I'll show her the jar of 2p coins I've been saving to use in the arcade. Just like last year, and the year before. It'll go too quickly and then I'll be back to posting letters. Redbrick house after redbrick house. Elastic bands, and sweat marks on the collar. Working on my tan from the knee down.

May turns away from me, kicking the duvet off her feet. Warm air from the window. The actual hoot of an actual bloody owl. I sing into her neck: '*She's a good-hearted woman in love with a good-timing man.*'

'Bugger off,' she says.

I kiss her ear. Awake all of a sudden. Not wanting to sleep.

She sighs, 'you won't remember any of this in the morning, you know.'

I hum the next line and move my hands down over her hips.

'I will,' I say, 'I bloody will.'

9:42 am

They only think about themselves. I could tell them
a thing or two. I could –
     if they stopped putting these   whatsits   all
over the place, don't need the things
     on my knees   don't need them everywhere. I like
a straight back. I like to be able to see   in the corners   in
the   dark places   behind

                                       trees and feathers
and bird's eggs   he brought
messages

I see the stars, I hear the rolling thunder   I want to hear
the music but

     there are people talking on the watching thingy
        talking and clapping and shouting their
uncouth ways.   Why
        would anyone want to see this when there
is so much

more

the boy, the boy, the boy. The sun in his hair as he
runs to the trees
there are

more things in heaven and earth

18 June 2003

Alex

So we drive. Out into the Forest of Bowland. Humid air, empty road, fingers tight on the wheel round each corner. It's national speed limit but I can't go over forty without feeling out of control. The corners are all sharper than they look. It's too hot. I'll be drenched before we get there.

'Not far now,' Lorna says, 'we need music.' She reaches across to the radio and I push her hand away.

'Don't. Need to concentrate.'

The gear crunches. She laughs. 'You're crapping yourself aren't you, Alex? The road of death. It'll be better once it's over. Face your fears and all that.'

'Yeah, yeah.'

She messes with her hair. Wind blowing through the car. I can smell shampoo, her perfume, something exotic. I can smell myself too, sweat and deodorant. The hedges and the farmhouse and the sign splattered with dried mud warning me to be careful of tractors turning. Lorna reaches into the backseat to get a book from the top of the pile. One of her shoestring gap-year guidebooks. Her tanned arm brushes against mine. White and freckled as anything. My shoulders hurt. A quick look in the rear-view mirror. There's a black Focus hovering up my backside ready to overtake. *Let them go,* the instructor would say, *they were all learners once you know.* But I'm not a learner anymore and it's embarrassing. I put my foot down.

'What do you think about hiring a car?' she says.

'I've already got a car.'

'Not here, you dick. Australia. If we go, I mean. Look –' she shoves the book towards me. I look down for a second. Windswept beach, white surf, crumbling cliffs.

'Great Ocean Road,' she announces, as though she already owns it, 'it's do-able in a couple of days with a car. Then you can head up to Darwin for some real heat.'

'Real heat? What's this then? Imitation?'

'You know what I mean. God, your knuckles are even whiter than normal.'

'Get lost, Lorna, I need to concentrate.'

She goes back to her book. I don't know how she can read in the car like that. It's making me sick just thinking about it. But then she's never ill. She's immortal. Never misses school, not like me – skiving at any opportunity, missing every school trip since year seven. And now I'm thinking about it: the Skipton Castle disaster. Sitting right at the front of the coach with newspaper on my knees, sucking on an extra-strong mint, biting my lips together, trying to keep my eyes fixed on something solid in the distance. A tree, a house, a road-sign, again and again and again. That rolling feeling in your guts, rising up, coming in waves. And someone calling me a ginger mong in the car park when I was gulping in fresh air, kicking their foot against my foot. *Where'd you get your shiny shoes from ginge?*

Ninety-nine p from the Paki-man shop? Knocking against me on purpose, stabbing their elbows into my back. *They should've put newspaper on the seat as well. You still piss the bed don't you Alex?'*

But it's all fields now. There's nothing to fix your eyes on. Just green and sky. I can't be sick now, can't relax, can't take my eyes off the road.

'Don't miss the turning,' she says, 'it's coming up any minute.'

'I know, I know.'

I slow down. It feels like I'm doing it too early, indicating when I'm still miles away like a spaz, but when it comes to it I almost overshoot. Gravel flies up and the hedge grazes the passenger side.

'Smooth, Alex,' she says, 'really smooth.'

'I thought you were here as support.'

'No – I'm here to talk about the trip.'

'If we're still alive at the end of this I'll be all yours.'

'Stop being such a drama queen.'

But this road is crazy. It's Russian roulette. Every corner is blind. Overgrown hedges on either side, twisting at ridiculous angles, only enough room for one car at a time, full of potholes and ditches. And this car doesn't feel like mine yet. It still smells of Nan's perfume. I stay in third gear and pray no one comes from the opposite direction. Lorna starts whistling something and I can't be bothered to tell her to stop.

'Whoa!' she says, 'what the hell is that?'

I brake. There's a game bird waddling out of the hedge, running like a divvy, a streak of colour on its head. I stop to let it go.

'Grouse,' I say, although I'm not really sure. I'm just changing back into first then there it is: a battered Land Rover coming towards us fast, braking just before it hits us.

'Bugger.'

'Go past him, Alex. He's waiting for you.'

I look at the space. My face getting hot. I could probably just do it, scrape by with one wheel in the ditch. There's no mud to get stuck in. All those times driving down the double-parked streets in town and the instructor saying, 'Don't look at the cars, look at the gap.' Land Rover man is holding his hand up. *What are you waiting for?* I check the rear-view mirror. There's a passing place a few metres back. It's safer. I start to put the car into reverse. My hand slipping off the gearstick.

'For God's sake, Alex. Make a decision will you?'

I steer the car backwards snaking from side to side, checking the mirrors again and again. As soon as there's room the other car accelerates and passes, tiny stones hitting the windscreen, my fingers shaking.

I drive. I don't look at her. I want to tell her to shut up but she hasn't said anything. The air is just loaded with it, with her face and the swallowed laughter, and her knowing me so well and expecting nothing more or less.

'It could be a nice little metaphor, if you think about it,' she says.

'I don't want to think about it though.'

'What is *with* you today? Maybe this was a bad idea.'

'Maybe.'

I park on a grass verge next to a farm gate. The field is most probably private but I don't care.

'Is this decisive enough for you?' I say.

She shrugs and piles the books back into her canvas bag. I grab the food. The car door slams. She pushes herself up over the gate first. I try not to look at her legs, muscled from years of long distance running and netball and inexhaustible energy. She sits down under a tree, back straight like a yoga instructor, and I sit next to her with my back against the trunk, right in the shade. Look up. The rough-grooved bark against my scalp, the light filtering through the little oval leaves, fanned out, barely moving. It's an ash. I can still remember the shapes from the *Pocket Guide to Trees* Nan bought me the year before high school, we used to go out, her and me and I would actually carry the bloody thing around so I could tick off every one I identified.

The plastic bag rustles as Lorna roots around for the sandwich without tomatoes in it. We eat. We surround ourselves with debris. We pretend not to be pissed off with each other. The grass is parched, scattered with buttercups, the sour, animal smell of cowpat or sheep crap or manure from somewhere nearby. She dabs sun cream on her nose, twists her hair up. For a minute I think she might ask me to do the back of her neck.

'I'm going to finish the plan and then we can talk about it – ok?'

'Fine.'

I lean back and close my eyes and try not to think about

her neck or anything else. I replace her with darkness, spring rain and mud. Jumping off the stile not so far from here in my green wellies with Nan. Sticking to the official routes, the rough wooden markers, the trampled-in paths in the corner of fields, over hills and cloughs and unexpected bridges. There were always sheep. I used to find them funny – bleating insults to each other like miserable old men, bellies hanging down ready to flood the place with spring clichés. She stopped me by the river once when I was busy looking down at the boggy ground, trying not to get sucked under.

'Shhh,' she said, 'the old man's sleeping.'

I squinted over the stone wall, my heart going fast, expecting to see a dirty tramp or a man with a beard made of moss, half buried. There was no one there.

'Not that way, up and across,' she said, pointing out to the fells, out over the fields behind the next farm. It was the nearest hill she meant. She crouched down and traced the shape of it for me. 'Can't you see him there lying on his back? He's sleeping off his dinner.'

I couldn't at first, it was just another bit of landscape, but then there was his beer belly, the dip of a neck, the outline of a chin, the blurred profile of his sleeping face. I held my breath and there was nothing but the sound of lapwings calling. I swear I saw his stomach move. I thought of Granddad, probably sleeping, himself. Laid out on the sofa. His belly all disappeared, his cheeks starting to sink. He'd said he didn't want to come, that walking was something he did for money not pleasure. But it was a lie because I remembered him coming when I was younger, before he got tired. I remembered him leading the way.

Nan was shading her eyes from a sudden bust of sunlight, still looking across the old man.

'His hair grows back curly every spring,' she said and I saw the promise of it in the new green leaves, the mass of trees around his head, running along his spine.

'Maybe by autumn it'll be the same colour as yours.'

'Are you asleep?'

'No.' I open my eyes and everything's too bright. She's kneeling now, sitting on her feet, holding a piece of paper.

'Ok. So I've finished it. I've tried to be as detailed as possible, but we can be flexible when we're out there. Nothing's set in stone.' She hands it to me and I scan down the list of dates and places. Thailand, Laos, Cambodia. Places I can't ever really picture myself going.

'Well?'

'It's very… thorough.'

'Alex.' The way she says it. She moves forward so her face is too close. Her eyes examining mine, moving like she's skim reading, summing things up, identifying the problem. Her eyes are flecked with green. Freckles on the bridge of her nose. Fuck. I'm fifteen again, in her room, leaning in too close, misreading all the signals. I'm going to do something stupid.

I stand up.

'I mean, do you even *want* to go anymore?'

'Of course.'

'Then what's the problem? Is it money? I can lend you some. You could pay me back when you've done some extra shifts at the pub.'

What is my problem? What the hell is wrong with me? I want to lie down under this tree forever. I'm everything and nothing. I matter and I don't. There has to be more. *Then sings my soul.* I want to be the old man, sleeping after a good meal and a pint. I want to be Rip Van Winkle. To dream for a thousand years then wake up with a badass beard, half buried in leaves and dried mud. The smell of sap and shit. The flutter of the ash tree. How am I supposed to explain that? If I say anything she'll piss herself. She'll say *Are you having one of your Lawrencian moments Alex?* She'll suck in her cheeks and raise an eyebrow. That word. She's been using it since *Sons and Lovers* last year in English, since I made the mistake of commenting on the blue-bells under the trees at the edge of the running track.

'Ah!' she said, gripping my arm, 'the long, blue cavernous bells that broke upon us like the aftermath of a beautiful flood.'

'What?'

'Very Lawrencian, Alex.'

And she explained it to me in detail. Defined the term like I was five and she was the Fountain of all Cultural Knowledge.

'For someone who hates Lawrence, you're suspiciously good at quoting him.'

'I can't help it. What woman could? He seduces me with language. He makes me long to be a sacrifice. I look up to him with dark dilating eyes.'

I look at her. 'I'm knackered,' I say. It's the best I can do.

She picks up one of the travel books and rolls her eyes. 'Have a nap then if it'll put you in a better mood. We need to make some decisions soon though. We need to sort the flights out.'

'I know.'

I take my shoes off and roll up my jeans, lie down with my arms behind my head and my feet in the sun. I close my eyes but I don't sleep. I think about her, I always think about her. The first time we spoke in high school. A storeroom in the music department. It was raining. Icy, blood-splintering rain. No way I was going out at break time. The prefects patrolled the corridors and checked the toilets. There weren't many places left to hide. Down some dim steps, strip lights flickering. I went in to the storeroom backwards to check no one was following. I didn't see her at first. She coughed to announce herself. I jumped and hit my head on the doorjamb.

'Come to join the resistance?' She held out a packet of chewing gum like it was a case of cigarettes and she was a film noir bombshell. Her hair was up. Her eye makeup black and smudged.

'Cheers,' I said and took a piece and started chewing. I couldn't believe my luck.

'Is someone after you?' she said.

'You never know with the Stasi, they'll stop at nothing.'

She laughed.

I made her laugh.

'If they find us we could always get the recorders out.' She pointed to the plastic storage box on the shelf above her head.

'An ideal torture method.'

'You have to pick the tunes carefully for maximum effect.'

'Morning Has Broken?'

'Good choice.'

'He's Got the Whole World in His Hands?'

'You're on my wavelength, soldier.'

People looked at me differently after I started hanging out with Lorna. The rich girl who managed to get herself expelled from boarding school. There were rumours. She had currency. My value went up just by association. Sometimes, when people assumed we were an item she'd ham it up. She'd put her arm round me and pull me in and say, 'you won't believe it, but actually we met in a cupboard! And we've never looked back, have we darling?'

And that's what we were, when I think about it. A unit. I know she was taking the piss, but that's how it felt. Us on the bench in the playground watching all the others. Footballers, terrified first years, girls rolling their skirts up at the waist and obsessing over twats who couldn't give a shit about them.

'It's so depressing,' Lorna said, 'imagine in ten years time what they'll all be doing. Working at the local chippy or a supermarket or the stinking cheese factory round the corner. Having babies and settling here without ever seeing anything, watching soaps every night and getting rat-arsed at the week-end to forget how sad their little lives are.'

I didn't say anything.

'After college I'm going travelling. Six months discovering the world then six months working for a charity in Africa or Thailand or anywhere. You should come.'

'Yeah.' I said it without thinking. What was there to think about?

'Who knows,' she said, 'maybe we'll never come back.'

I squint through the sunlight. The high grass swishing by the gate. A crow landing on a fence post. Its harsh call is like a warning, like a sound effect from a horror film.

I can still hear Lorna's pen scratching across the page of her notebook. I don't look at her. None of this feels real anymore. It feels like tagging along. I hardly see her in the week and when I wait to give her a lift it's like I'm dragging her away from her real friends, the grammar school kids with their mobiles, low-cut jeans and platforms sandals. And the guy who's always giving her the eye. She giggles. It's embarrassing. Her voice is different. Like she's trying to bleach the north-ern-ness out of it. I can just imagine her with him at the club in town wearing a short skirt, shuffling around to the Euro-bland dance music we've always hated, and him in a bog-standard checked going-out shirt moving in for a snog. So predictable. The thought of her wasting time with a guy like that. The thought of me going away with her somewhere hotter than this. Right now, anywhere other than this is unimaginable.

When Nan met her for the first time she told me to be careful, she said if I didn't watch myself Lorna would have me for breakfast. She was already losing it then. But she still knew who I was. She hadn't started acting like I was invisible.

I pick at the grass in handfuls and let it drop. Everything smells like life. Wispy clouds moving across the sky. Blur my eyes and stare long enough and they could be old men or game birds or anything. Nan and me sheltering from rain under the pale green metal bridge. She told me it was really an aqueduct. She told me about boggarts and trolls, that there had been more sightings in this little corner of Lancashire than in any place in Britain.

'They live under bridges,' she said, 'but don't worry, they never come out in the rain.'

'Wake up,' Lorna says, 'come on, time to plan.'

She sounds like my mother. So bloody eager I can't stand it.

'I just don't feel like it today.'

'Then what the hell are we doing here?'

I sit up. 'Look at this place. How can you even think about Australia here?'

'My mistake. I didn't realise we were here to appreciate nature. Is that what we're doing then, Alex? Soaking up the deep *fecund* essence of the earth?'

She's grinning at me. I get up, grab my shoes, my rucksack.

'Alex?'

I walk quickly across the field, ignoring the sharp stones and twigs, and all but hurdle the metal gate.

On the way home we sit in silence. Her knees are clamped together, angled away from me. She looks out the window. I drive down the hill, past the pub and the church, into the quiet, middle class suburb she's so desperate to escape. It's easy to leave when you've got money. It's easy to go on an adventure when you know exactly what you'll be coming back to.

I turn into her drive, watching the gap, not the gateposts, and we sit there for a few seconds. She unclicks her seatbelt.

'You're not coming are you?'

'I don't think so, no.'

She nods, staring forward. Her voice sounds strange and neutral. My heart beating loud in my ears.

'What will you do?'

I shrug, 'Probably just, you know, stay here and appreciate nature.'

A twitch at the corner of her mouth. She reaches for her bag out of the back seat and sits there for a moment. She leans across the gearstick quickly, holds my face and kisses me. A 1940s film-star kiss. I don't have time to feel anything.

'Goodbye, Alex.'

She doesn't look back. I watch her turning the key, the sharpness of her elbow, her knee pushing against the door where it sticks. Her hair tangled from the drive. She's gone. I imagine her slumped against the door, sobbing silently on the other side next to the executive umbrellas and shoes neatly lined up in the rack, the hallway that smells of polished wood and expensive washing powder. But that's all it is. A fantasy.

The windows are all clean and blank. The lawn is neatly edged. There are red geraniums in terracotta pots.

This image burns into me. I'll remember it just as it is.

10:35 am

      but that wasn't the point after all because
Mum said he already had a mother and so we shouldn't
meddle

      but his mother had bruises on top of her bruises
and it was Dad's job to

          sort things out   because there are bad
men.

So he went, and he went again.

And sometimes the boy still came to the door and he was
never

      dressed   right   and then

               we spoke of many things,

many things   but not with
words.

        Sunlight right in my – and the dust   silver and
gold everywhere   I could touch it   if I –

Why do they never stop talking? Are they looking
are they looking at me?

Leaves and feathers and bottletops on the backstep. He was
trying to tell me
something

but they hide all my letters and smile while they do it.
        No stamps, no envelopes.
The doors are all locked. The messages never get through.

12 May 1999

Afsana

Gill unlocks the craft room. All her keys jangle as she tries to find the right one. Inside it smells like paint and new carpet. The walls are spotlessly white. She opens a window and a rush of fresh air cuts through the chemical smell. I can see the staff car park, the bus stop, the pink petals from the blossom trees clogging the drains along the main road. She puts her pile of papers and pens down on the metal table.

'We haven't used it much yet,' she says, 'but the relatives like to know we offer this kind of thing. And now you're here…'

It makes me feel a bit sick, the thought of her relying on me. Now I'm here I want to run in the other direction.

'You'll mainly be watching today of course, helping record what they say. Seeing how we do things. We'll be trying to work on their memory books and maybe gather some ideas for displays.'

I look at the pin board on the wall, half full of grainy photocopied images: an old-fashioned car, a church with the steeple cut off half way down, a group of women in 1950s dresses standing on a promenade. The photos are cut out and backed on coloured paper. All the stencilled letters are wonky.

'Ok, Sana?' she says.

'Fine.'

'You'll get the hang of things in no time.' She hands me a packet of cheap custard creams and a paper plate. 'Open these and I'll go and fetch the group.'

There's an empty notebook in front of my seat. And a pen. I didn't think about this when I applied. I thought about all the physical stuff. The hygiene training and everything. I prepared myself. Gill probably thinks she's easing me in gently. Just a little spot of writing.

I can hear them coming down the corridor. I lean on the table and try to look natural. Maybe Ewan was right. If I was really cut out for this I wouldn't be so scared.

'Sana, help Albert into his chair, will you?' Gill says.

She walks him in – her arm through his, and all the others follow on behind. It feels a bit formal. Like a procession. I'm so nervous I want to laugh. Nobody's talking. I take his arm and he smiles and pulls me in too close. His waistcoat is covered in tiny little dots. I steer him slowly round the top end of the table to the chair furthest from the door. He takes my hand and kisses it, like an actor in a film.

'Sana, this is Malcolm, Tony and May. May's still feeling a little unsettled, aren't you, love?'

'Unsettled is the least of it,' Malcolm says banging his fist on the table. He has a Scottish accent. Even sitting down he's massive. Tall and bulky and impossible to ignore. 'Unsettled is the tip of the bloody iceberg.'

He looks at me.

'What's your name again, hen?'

'Afsana.'

'Afsana. Af. Sana. Well, that's a new one.' He angles his chair away from Gill and leans across the table. 'What is it we're doing here, Afsana? What are we waiting for? What's expected?'

I sit down next to May who mutters something under her breath. Before I can answer him Gill steps in. 'Life stories, Malcolm,' she doesn't look up, 'we're sharing memories.'

'Well in that case let's start at the beginning. Picture it: The Glasgow slums, nineteen…. nineteen…,' he waves his hands around and almost hits Tony in the head, 'oh, sod it. A bloody long time ago. One cold morning when the rain is shitting down, a baby slips out of its mother a month too early. Slips out of her like a mackerel from the Clyde.'

Gill sighs. 'It's Tony's turn now, Malcolm, we're listening to Tony's memories.' She reaches out and touches Tony's sleeve. He jumps a little and looks up, adjusts his glasses, tries to focus. 'That's right, isn't it, love. You remember? We were talking about where you met your wife, Jean.'

He clears his throat. 'Willerton Conservative Club 1952. A tea dance. She was wearing a blue dress and I—'

'A Tory, eh! I might've known. I can tell by the way you wear your glasses. Blue was the right colour for her then. Appropriate. I bet it was buttoned right up to the top.'

'No politics, Malcolm. You know the rules. If you start you'll have to leave the group.'

Malcolm pretends to zip his lips together. He winks at me. I look away. On the other side of me May is rocking gently, staring at her hands, rubbing them together. She leans closer. 'I had a dress with blue buttons,' she says, 'I wore it in the tea tent.'

Tony looks bewildered. Albert has already put his head down on the table and fallen asleep.

'A blue dress, Tony?' Gill prompts.

'And I asked her to dance...'

'Of course you did,' Malcolm says, 'It was the logical next step.'

'A quickstep.'

'No use in hesitating.' Malcolm stands up and gets into the ballroom position, as if he's ready for a partner. 'Come on, Tory boy. Don't keep a lady waiting.'

'Sit down, Malcolm.'

He does, but somehow, in the confusion, May has pushed her chair back and is halfway towards the door. By the time I catch up with her and take her arm she's shaking. Humming a tune under her breath as if her life depends on it.

'It's ok,' I tell her guiding her back to the table, 'let's just sit back down with the others.'

'Come on then, Tony, tell us more about this dance. We're just dying to hear all the details. Did she let you get fruity? Did she let you undo some of those buttons by the end?' Malcolm leans forward and cups his ear. Tony shrugs and looks at Gill for guidance.

'*To everything there is a season,*' May says to her hands '*a time to weep, a time to mourn, a time to laugh—*'

'Would you credit it?' Malcolm says to no one in particular, 'a Tory *and* a God-botherer. Please, won't someone just get me the fuck out of here?'

'Language, Malcolm.'

Albert wakes up and sits upright as though someone has just stuck a pin in his arm. 'What's happening?' he says too loudly, 'what are you saying? What have I missed?'

'Jesus Christ!'

'Really?' Albert looks around, scans our faces for confirmation. 'Really? I was sure that was only a dream.'

There are footsteps outside. Someone running down the corridor towards us. Keys jangling. Gill looks up. Alison is at the door, out of breath and gripping onto the frame.

'You're needed,' she says to Gill, her eyebrows raised.

'Sorry, Tony,' Gill says and then 'Sana – you're going to have to take over in here – just for ten minutes or so. Then you can take them into the dining room for tea.'

'Ok,' I say, 'no problem. That's fine.' The words just slip out of me. Really I want to grab hold of her hand and force her to stay. But she's gone and May is rocking next to me and Malcolm looks like all his birthdays have come at once. He moves into Gill's seat before I can say anything and taps her pen on the table. He reaches across and takes three biscuits from the plate.

'What song did you dance to, Tory boy?' he says through a mouthful of crumbs.

Tony hesitates. He looks anxious. He glances at me and I nod for him continue.

'The Very Thought of You,' he says, 'it was always our song and we danced to it at our wedding.'

I try to write it in the notebook. It's the kind of detail Gill's looking for. May's whispering next to me. Something about a boy. I can't concentrate. I don't know the song and I've half forgotten the title already.

'Was it swish, Tory boy? Were you just drowning in champagne?'

'What?' Tony says. 'What's that?'

'I can't hear anything either,' Albert shouts, 'not a bloody thing.'

Malcolm stands up again and starts to sing. *The very thought of you*. His voice is deep and gravelly. Slightly off key. It doesn't match the words. He sounds like the football fans who used to fill the streets near ours after matches. I should stop him really. I should try to bring things back in line. But Albert seems happy for the first time today. He starts to hum, murmurs the words along with Malcolm and then takes over.

'I'm living in a kind of daydream. I'm happy as can be, and, foolish as it may seem, to me that's everything...'

He sings the whole verse and chorus while Malcolm conducts with the pen. His voice is all 1940s. Smooth and rich. Like Gene Kelly or Fred Astaire. And May has stopped rocking now, finally. Her hands aren't clenched. She stares up at the newly painted ceiling. For just a minute her face is full of peace. Everything is suspended. And I can't help thinking of Mum ironing in the living room on a Saturday afternoon. We'd watch musicals and old films. Just me and her. Amina out with a friend or upstairs reading romance novels smuggled in from the library. I'd dance and try to do handstands against the armchair. Once at mosque, someone had claimed that music was haram except in prayer. Except for voices raised in du'a. Amina had nudged me and rolled her eyes but she didn't say anything. I wanted to ask Baba about it but I was too scared. I practised the argument in my head, the one I never had the courage to speak out loud. Surely even the Prophet (peace be upon him) liked to dance every now and then? I wanted a lilac dress like Debbie Reynolds in *Singin' in the Rain*. Standing on a stepladder in the empty sound stage while Gene Kelly turns on all the lights and the smoke and the wind, so that the billowy bits of her dress blow back. He sings into her face. I wanted to stand on the back of the sofa and balance and let it roll over onto its side while singing and smiling as if it was the easiest thing in the world.

'What's your name, hen?' Malcolm says quietly.

'Afsana.'

'I used to have a dress with blue buttons,' May says, 'I wore it at the field day to serve the tea.'

'Do you fancy a dance, Afsana?' Malcolm puts on a posh voice, 'will you do me the honour of taking a turn about the room?'

I shake my head. I need to establish some authority. Tony takes his glasses off and massages the bridge of his nose. He puts them back on and squints at the window, noticing something, half standing up to get a better look. And now Malcolm's seen it too. I turn in my chair and there's an ambulance pulling into the car park. A quick burst of lights, a flash of yellow and green.

'Fuck me,' Malcolm says to nobody in particular. 'The bastards! Who've they done away with this time?'

After lunch I hover in the day room. Gill is nowhere to be seen. The other staff come in and deal with toilet trips and refills and then disappear. Nobody gives me any instructions. May beckons me closer and I kneel by her chair so she can whisper.

'Mum let me serve the tea,' she says counting each statement off on her fingers, 'I wore the dress with the blue buttons. I saw him running into the trees. Such a little thing. And he never came back. They won't let me out to find him. But you understand.' She looks at me, so directly, so full of pleading. 'They say he doesn't talk but he speaks to me. I read things in his eyes. You understand, don't you?'

I don't have time to answer. Alison is coming towards me from the kitchen. Two paramedics stride through the corridors and out the front entrance.

'If you see him you'll tell him where I am?' she says.

'There you are, Sana. Have you managed to have a break yet?'

'No. I'm sorry. I wasn't sure—'

She waves away my apology, 'we're going to have to finish your training tomorrow, I'm afraid.'

'Ok.'

She rubs her hand over her eyes and beckons for me to follow her out into the corridor.

'There was a death,' she says, in a whisper, 'Flora. A sudden stroke. Gill's trying to contact the family before we release the body and there's paperwork. Everything's up in the air.'

I try to picture Flora, try to remember if I was ever introduced. 'What do you need me to do?'

'There's one thing,' she says, 'you can say no if it's too much.'

'Anything.'

'Can you sit with her? Make sure the room's straight and clean, make sure she's got her dignity for when her relatives arrive?'

I nod. There are noises from the day room now. A woman is screaming. There are groans. Someone shouts something about wanting to go home.

She squeezes my arm, 'I'd better go and sort that rabble out,' she opens the door and we both wince at the noise. 'Room twelve,' she says, then disappears.

The quiet is such a relief that I don't have time to be scared. Flora is laid out on the bed with her eyes closed. I kneel on the floor and lean over her. Pull the covers higher, right up to her neck, and straighten out the sheets. Her hair is thin and yellowy. Her skin looks grey, like concrete. I think of my mother in the hospital, nearing the end and how Baba wouldn't let us see her after she was gone. He kept us away from all of it. He could barely speak. He shut himself into the study and wrote letters and waited for his mother to arrive.

I asked Amina what they would do with her body.

'Wash it,' she said, 'and wrap it and bury it.'

'Wrap it in what?'

'I don't know'.

'Will they pray for her?'

'Of course.'

'Which prayers will they say?'

'I don't know, Sana. Stop asking questions and leave me alone.'

But I couldn't stop the questions. They stayed in my head. I wanted to know who would be touching her and what would happen if they did it wrong, and how long she would have to lie in the wet earth until judgement. I wanted someone to tell me which gate of Jannah she would be allowed through when the time came. I imagined her rolled tight with strips of white cloth, like an Egyptian Mummy, and I couldn't get to sleep at night. In the dark I could hear Baba speaking on the phone downstairs and the sound of Amina's bed creaking every time she rolled over.

This room is already clean and neat. There's nothing much for me to do. So I sit down. Flora's forehead is creased, like she's searching for an answer, like death has interrupted something. I think about heaven – the way it's always so white and blinding, in films and on TV. Like the tiles in all the bathrooms here. Like the new paint in the craft room. Ewan doesn't believe in an afterlife. We should live in the here and now, not hold out for rewards that may or may not be real, he says. It's like a drug – all of it. It's just another form of control.

I reach out and touch her – fingertip to fingertip. I dare myself. She is somewhere else. She has to be. I wish her an afterlife full of colour. I wish her fountains and Persian rugs, flower gardens and dresses finished with gold thread. I wish her some tender meat and a better brand of gravy.

On the bus home I press my nose against the glass and feel the vibrations of the engine through my whole body. I tune everything out. Tonight it's antipasti. Ewan wants to celebrate the turn in the weather, to revisit memories of his gap year in Tuscany. *One day we'll go there*, he says sometimes, *I'll take you on a tour. We'll taste the wine from the vineyard where I picked grapes until my fingers bled*. He'll pick the stuff up from the deli on the way home from work. He'll lay out the strips of ham and salami in contrasting stripes and I'll try not think about what Baba would say if he could see me. Sliced bread and the coffee table filled with bowls of herby rice and grilled vegetables swimming in oil. He'll put an olive onto my plate and remind me that some tastes are acquired. *This one was grown on an ancient tree in the shadow of Mount Etna*, he'll say, or something like that. He'll hold the fork out and watch my face as I bite it. He finds it funnier every time.

Past the roundabout, the retail park, the takeaways. A hot whiff of spices through the open window. I close my eyes.

The week after Mum died I couldn't sleep. I crept downstairs. Dadi was in the kitchen pouring chickpeas into a bowl of salted water. The kitchen smelled different already. I wanted toast and jam or the special crisps with the separate pouch of salt to shake. Dadi had filled the cupboards with strange food with labels I couldn't read. Big packets of flour and sacks of onions. She told me to hush when she saw I was crying. She gave me a glass of water and turned me around.

'Tomorrow you help me make chole,' she said, pushing me back up the stairs, 'busy hands are better than tears.'

In the morning she stood over me while I toasted cardamom, cumin seeds and cinnamon in a pan. She told me how many peppercorns were too much. We made the paste and the gravy, we simmered and stirred. It felt like hours standing over the heat and steam. I wondered how women like Dadi ever managed to do anything else.

My stomach rumbles but the sound is swallowed by the noise of the engine and the beat of a song escaping from someone's headphones at the back of the bus. I didn't like it then but I could eat it now. Imagine her putting the bowl in front of me again. The sauce and sliced onions, the puffed up bhatura, the warmth of the spices mixed with snot and tears. I could tell Ewan that somebody asked me to dance today and somebody died. I could leave the ham and olives on my plate.

The sun streams in through the window and I have to cover my eyes. Somebody rings the bell before I get a chance to. I reach down to gather my bags. I'll tell Ewan it was all fine. Then I'll sleep. I'll go back tomorrow. One day at a time. I'll finish my training at the very least.

11:05 am

if its not too much to ask I'd like to   I just want to
say there's

      something
           cooking. I just want to get clean.

           Mum scrubs my fingernails. There's no use
complaining. She shows me lots of things. How to roll the
pastry outwards. How to find the right –

people   always blathering about. No gumption. Not an
ounce between them.

   Move this, go here, don't open that door.

   The kind of people who make gravy from a packet, and
don't strain it properly.

They don't even ask my advice.

Close your eyes and they think you're asleep and they leave
you be.

           Too many voices.

             She said lipstick is for them who
want to advertise. The light of God needs no   assistance.

   But these buttons are coming loose and I haven't got a

needle. The devil is in the details. The devil is in

these buttons. Coming loose.

Some of these people in here, they've got nothing going on up top. These women. If I had a pin   I know
       where   I know what

       I want

5 September 1983

Karen

Claire isn't standing by the kiosk like she said. She promised she'd come straight from work so I wouldn't have to walk through the underpass alone. I can't see her anywhere so I buy a packet of chewing gum and sit on the long bench opposite the bus stands, keeping my legs crossed tight. Goose pimples. The wind is cold, blowing through the gaps in the sliding doors. Little spots of rain catching on the glass. All the separate sections, the big white numbers, the people waiting in their dowdy clothes, weighed down with shopping bags, ready to go home for a chippy tea. I get my compact out and check my teeth for lipstick smudges. The colour seems brighter than it did at home. I try to blot it on the back of my hand. The woman at the counter was adamant it was the right shade for my skin tone. Smile into the mirror and think of Dad's face when he bumped into me in the hallway.

'Bloody hell, Karen, what's the occasion?'

'Nothing special.'

'Are you sure you haven't forgotten the rest of that dress?'

'It's fashion, Dad.'

I pushed past him into the kitchen. Mum was standing at the sink, her hands covered in bubbles. She looked like a bloody Fairy Liquid advert.

'Can I borrow the spare key, I've lost mine.'

'Again?' she said and turned round. She hesitated for a second, looked me up and down, her mouth going tight.

'What?' I said, all defensive, already anticipating the comments. 'What are you staring at?'

'Altogether too much,' she said, 'but I doubt it's me you were trying to impress.'

She doesn't even try to get me to go to the church hall disco anymore. She'd be ashamed for all her cronies to see what kind of daughter she's raised.

'The key,' I said, holding out my hand.

'In the top drawer.'

She turned around and went straight back to her pots and pans.

I close the compact and the whole place seems bigger and emptier. The big clocks hanging down and ticking the seconds off my life one by one. Buses have come and gone and it's starting to go dark. I can hear a group of men coming up from the underpass. Shouting and messing about. They sound like football fans after a win. Drunk and hyped up, on the verge of doing something stupid. It's the last time I trust Claire to do anything. I push myself back into the bench as far as I can and pretend to look for something in my bag. The voices get louder and then stop. I can see them out the corner of my eye. One moving mass.

'Hey, hey, hey!'

'Alright sweetheart?'

'Budge up, Love, there's room for everyone.'

I've got no choice. There's four of them. Two on either side of me. They sit down and hem me in. Their legs brushing against mine even though the bench is still half empty.

'Where you off to tonight then?'

I want to ignore them but it'll make things worse. They can feel my fear. They're feeding on it.

'I'm meeting a friend.'

'Been stood up, have yer?'

'Eh? It's a disgrace, that. A sexy bird like you without a date.'

'Come out with us. We're off to the docks. The Manxman. You know it?'

'I've heard of it.'

'You don't get seasick do you? You don't mind a bit of rocking on a Friday night?' He bumps into my shoulder so I fall against the bloke on the other side.

'Watch it, Tommy,' he says, 'stop being such a fucking knob.'

I hold my bag in front of me and stand up. 'I'm off now,' I say, 'have a good night.' I start walking but one of them grabs my wrist and pulls me back.

'Hey!'

He won't let go. Clinging onto my arm while he slides down onto the floor, onto his knees, right against me. I can feel his breath on my legs. I grab my dress at the back and pull it as tight as I can. His fingers digging into my arm and the others laughing or whistling or turning their bastard faces away so they don't have to intervene.

'Let. Go.'

I try to pull away but he's not having any of it. I can hear a bus pulling in to a space nearby and pray it's full of people.

'I will,' he says, 'believe me. But first I have to say this. This might seem a bit sudden...'

'Tommy, you absolute wanker,' someone says laughing, 'you can't propose to every girl with a nice pair of legs.'

'What's going on?'

A new voice coming from the other direction. Tommy lets go of my arm and I stand back. There's a row of red marks where his nails were digging in.

'You alright, love?' the man says moving in front of me, looking back and forth. He's wearing a navy polo shirt with a white stripe at the collar. Tall and wiry with close cropped fair hair. His jeans all dusty at the knees.

'These idiots bothering you were they?'

I nod and Tommy stands up, tries to steady himself. He holds his hands up in surrender and the others don't know where to look.

'Just a bit of fun,' he says, 'no need for any trouble, mate.'

'It didn't look like she was having a lot of fun to me, sunshine. Four against one? Is that the only way you can manage to get yourself a woman?'

Someone laughs. Tommy's face is going pink. He puts his hands down and swipes behind him at whoever happens to be in line.

The man turns back to me. 'Going home or into town?'

I hesitate. Just for a second, making my mind up. 'Town.'

He offers me his arm and if it wasn't for the scruffy clothes he could be a gentleman in one of Mum's Sunday night costume dramas. 'Come on then,' he says, 'I'll walk you in.'

The underpass slopes down into the gloom. The rubber floor tiles are all slippy from the rain. I hold onto the metal railing to steady myself and take it slow.

'Careful,' he says.

'I'm fine. It's just these heels.'

'It's not you, it's this bloody floor. See the way the grooves run from top to bottom?'

'Yeah.'

'The tiles were supposed to be laid horizontal – you know – across the grain, to create some resistance. Some idiot messed it up and now it's a bloody death trap.'

'How do you know?'

'My old man told me about it. It was in the papers not long after they built this place. But it's obvious really, when you think about it.'

'Is that what you do then – build things?'

He looks down at his jeans and back to me, he grins. 'I'm a plasterer,' he says, 'but I've got bigger plans. All I have to do is save up the cash.'

'What plans?'

'Nah,' he waves the question away, 'I won't bore you with the details.'

'Go on. I'm interested.'

'Really?' he says.'

I nod.

'Ok,' he stops walking, he runs his hand over his head, around the stubble on his chin. 'So I have this contact who works with big department stores all across the country, dealing in shop fittings, you know, shelving and mannequins and all that stuff.' He can't keep still. Moving back and forth the whole time, rocking on the balls of his feet.

'He'll let me have a load of stock on the cheap – good quality stuff that's been used a bit, just needs some attention. And I'll do it up and sell it on to smaller businesses – little boutiques that can't afford to get it new.'

I nod.

'That's about it,' he says. He shrugs and starts walking again.

'And then people like me can come along and buy our Friday night outfits in the luxury we deserve.'

He looks at me, really looks at me as though he can't work out whether I'm serious or not. Like he's seeing me for the first time. His pupils are all big in the dim yellow light.

'Where *does* a girl like you go on a Friday night dressed like that?'

'I was supposed to be meeting someone. We were going dancing. To Clouds or Scamps, maybe.'

'His loss.'

'It was a girlfriend, actually.'

'Oh,' he says and looks away, 'right.'

I stop and touch his arm. 'Not like that.'

He breathes out. 'Well thank God for that.'

We both laugh. We're coming out of the underpass now,

away from the graffiti and the smell of piss and into the open. The rain has stopped but the air is still damp with it. Water dripping from a shop awning onto the concrete steps.

'Look,' he says, 'I'm not really dressed for clubbing, but if you aren't scared of slumming it for a bit I'd love to buy you a drink before you head off.'

I follow him into the pub and the air is thick with smoke and testosterone. There's hardly a woman in sight. He finds us a table and goes to order the drinks. I don't even know his name. The walls are covered with old signs and coasters. It looks like a setting for a 1930s gangster movie. The brown and green tiles and the landlord working the beer taps like a pro. There's a big mirror hung behind the bar, edged with some kind of pattern and spotted with age. He catches me looking over as he's paying and his reflection smiles back. I wedge my handbag under the seat, behind my feet. Somebody laughs and bumps into the table as they push past. All the voices and singing, the sound of the darts hitting the board and the groans and the coins clinking as money changes hands.

'One Bacardi and Coke,' he says, putting the glass in front of me, 'and a packet of crisps so no one can say I didn't show you a good time.'

I laugh and hold my hand out. 'Karen,' I say, 'nice to meet you.'

'Bloody hell, you're right!' he puts his drink down and wipes his hand on his trouser leg, he shakes my hand and his grip is so firm it almost hurts. 'Ian.'

'Thanks for earlier, Ian.'

'What, those idiots?' he says, 'it was a pleasure.' He takes a sip of his beer.

I keep waiting for the dodgy chat up line, for a reason to leave after I finish this drink. But he doesn't try anything on. He doesn't say *nice legs, what time do they open?* or ask me if I bruised myself when I fell down from heaven. Nothing feels awkward.

He knocks a cigarette on the table. 'Do you mind?'

'No. Go ahead.'

He flicks at his lighter but before he can work up a flame a strange bloke slips onto the seat next to me, right next to me, and grabs a cigarette from Ian's packet.

'Hey!'

'Allo, allo, allo,' he says, like a comedy policeman from the telly, 'who do we have here then?'

Ian snatches the fag back out of his hand. 'Piss off, Langie.' His voice is all quiet and tight. The smile is long gone.

The man turns to me as if we're old friends. He smells of unwashed clothes and fried food. His face is all pockmarked and scabby; his head so small it looks like someone shrunk it in the wash. He's too close. I look at Ian and he shakes his head. He gives me a look as if to say he's sorry for whatever's about to come.

'I seen him coming down this way from the bus station,' Langie says to me, 'and I thought *that can't be my mate Ian can it?* Not when we was due to meet on the other side of town half an hour ago.'

'I told you I wasn't coming, I don't want nothing to do with any of it.'

'But now I can see you had a good excuse. If I had a bird like this on my arm I'd be forgetting appointments left, right and centre.'

'I'm telling you,' he hisses, 'now is not the time.'

Langie reaches down into a plastic bag. It's a white C&A one with the handles all stretched and almost breaking. He brings out a camera, a brand new Polaroid, and sets it on the table.

'There's more where this came from,' he says, looking at Ian, 'I just need to get the word out. You don't mind me testing it do you? Your girlfriend would make the perfect model.'

He points the camera at me and gets ready to take the shot. I put my hand over my face, lean away and Ian is half standing up, reaching over to grab it. He knocks my drink and I just manage to catch it before it spills. The flash goes off and Langie stands up, grinning, holding the camera just out of reach.

The photo appears out the bottom. A white square starting to go dark in the middle. Langie takes it out and wafts it in the air. I can't stop looking. There's something off about the way he smiles.

'Don't worry,' he says, 'I'll leave you two lovebirds alone.'

Ian glares at him. The muscles in his neck are twitching.

'I'll be in touch though, mate,' Langie says, 'we still have things to talk about, you and me.' He puts the camera back in the bag and drops the photo on the table before leaving.

Ian goes to pick it up but I get there first. Langie's managed to catch the edge of my arm, but nothing else. The camera must've been knocked away in all the commotion. The photo is all Ian. His eyes tinged with red. He looks like a completely different person.

'I'm sorry,' he says, pushing his stool back and starting to stand up, 'this was a bad idea.'

'No,' I catch his arm, 'don't go. Finish your drink at least.'

He sits back down. I watch him take a sip. He's knackered. I can see that now. He looks away, moving his pint glass from side to side so that the liquid sloshes around.

'Look at you,' he says finally and his voice is flat, 'you really shouldn't get yourself mixed up with someone like me.'

He sounds so sad. I say, 'Why don't you let me be the judge of that?'

'I'm sorry about Langie,' he says finally, 'he's an old friend. Well, not really a *friend*, you know? Just someone who used to hang out with my brother. Used to come round ours and scrounge sugar butties after school.'

'You have a brother?'

'Yeah. And two sisters. And a half sister somewhere over Blackburn way. I never see her. I try not to see any of them if I'm honest. They're all off their heads.'

'I always wanted a sister.'

'Right. But what I'm trying to say is – I used to be mixed up in all kinds of shit. I want to be straight with you because you're different. You're not–' he waves his hands around searching for a word.

'What?'

'I dunno. There's just something about you. I don't want to lie.'

He's looking at me, right into my eyes and I don't look away. This prickling down the back of my neck. I don't know if it's excitement or a warning.

It's turning into one of those nights. Everything blurring, the lights and the voices. Someone, somewhere laughing too loud. I tell Ian about work, the young lads trying to smuggle condoms out in their jacket pockets and Gary behind the photo counter who holds his magnifying glass up against all the negatives hoping for a topless sunbather in the back of someone's holiday shots. Ian's eyes screw up at the corners when he laughs. He's hanging on every word. I think about Mum's face when I told her I was dropping out of college to work full time at Boots. 'You'll regret it,' she said, shaking her head, 'just mark my words.' But I don't regret it. Writing essays about dead men from history who did things that don't matter anymore. I can't regret anything on a night like this, with a man like this, whose eyes are a new colour every time he blinks. It's not like he's even that good looking. But there's something about him, electricity in his fingertips. His hand brushes mine as he reaches for his glass and everything stops. I can't for the life of me remember what it was I was saying.

A bell rings and we both sit up.

'Last orders please, gentlemen!'

The pub is still heaving. Ian looks at his watch. 'No way. No way it's that time already.'

I stretch my legs out and roll my shoulders back. 'I've got work in the morning,' I say. 'Bloody Claire. Persuades me to come out and then can't even be bothered to turn up.'

'Some friend,' he says, 'where do you live?'

I tell him and he laughs. 'Seriously? We're almost neighbours then. I'm in the flat above the bookie's just round the corner.'

'Piss off!'

'I swear. Cross my heart and hope to die.'

'We should share a taxi then.'

He nods and stands up and has to steady himself on the table. 'I'm not drunk,' he says catching my eye, 'well, not *that* drunk. My knees are just seizing up.'

I laugh. He sounds just like Dad.

'It's not funny,' he says, but he's not really angry, 'you ask any plasterer. It knackers your body. Just one of the many reasons I need to move on.'

'You didn't seem so decrepit when you were rescuing me from that gang of violent thugs earlier.'

'Is that the way you're going to tell it?'

'That's exactly the way.'

He smiles.

I reach down for my bag and slip the photo into the front pocket when he's not looking.

And it's the sound of my heels on the pavement. His arm brushing against mine. His hand on the small of my back as we cross to the other side. The odd car swishing past on the wet roads. Music escaping from Scamps, the thud of the bass, the bouncers standing by the front door chewing gum and looking bored out of their skulls. We run for a taxi before the rush and the door slams shut on all the noise.

'Lane Ends please, mate,' he says.

I check my purse to get my money ready and Ian tells me to put it away. His face is all kindness now, soft and slack, not like before, not like in the photo. We drive past groups of people coming out of the pubs, lights on in windows and queues outside the takeaways by the polytechnic.

'Wait a minute,' I say, 'you never told me where you were actually planning to go tonight before I hijacked your evening.'

'It's not exciting. I was coming in from a job out Chorley way. I was going to walk to the other side of the station and get the next bus home.'

'So you weren't even going into town at all?'

'It's not like it was a hardship. You're a lot more exciting than dinner in front of the TV.'

I smile. There's a gentleness about him. It's surprising. With all the stuff he must have been through. All the violence and chaos. Making his way on his own. I get the feeling I've only begun to touch the surface.

The car stops at the lights near home. I open my bag and pretend to look for something, catch the sharp edge of the spare key on the palm of my hand.

'What number do you live at?' he says.

I hesitate. My street. Mum and Dad and all the others. Tucked in safely. Net curtains snug against the windows. The kind of life you end up with if you always play it safe. She'd say I'm playing with fire. She'd say people with that background always return to type in the end. The lights turn green. I lean across to whisper in his ear. He smells of paint and sweat and aftershave.

'I've forgotten my key,' I say, 'why don't we just go straight to yours?'

12:15 am

because nobody will tell me what it is I'm expected to do. There'll be a backlog at the Post Office before long. They'll know something's up because I'm never

and I can't think how to get a message through. No one will give me any stamps.

The ink runs and the letters get mixed up. All the
Words   words   words
                they never stay put.

The birds try to get in.
       Not the right kind   for carrying messages.
No one has given me the code. One for sorrow, two for sorrow
       all that peck, peck pecking on the glass.

They say he wandered very far, very far –
and who can blame him? There's no green. There's nothing here for children.

I have to keep singing   *A little shy,   and sad of eye,
and very wise*

but not wise enough to stay out of the trees, to stay away

from the water.

   Dad must have found him by now. Mum said there
are so many miracles but I'm still waiting for the
        wonders   and

28 November 1989

Arthur

If I wake him up there'll be hell to pay. I can hear May in the kitchen opening the cupboards, sifting flour and cocoa powder into the big bowl, performing everyday magic with sugar and eggs. It's already dark outside. Alex lying on the sofa. Tuck his skinny little legs back in under the blanket. His mouth hanging open. The rise and fall of his chest. Rain against the window and the gas fire ticking away, pumping that drowsy heat at us, turning his cheeks pink. I hope he's dreaming about something exciting. Discovering a cave full of treasure and riding on an elephant through the streets with the crowds all cheering him on. I want to pick him up and squeeze all the fear away. I want to tell him it'll be alright. Kneeling here next to the sofa like it's an altar, like I'm about to plead for divine help. If anyone could make me do it, he could. Right this minute I'd pray properly for the first time since school assembly and ask for protection, ask for all the memories of his shit of a father to be rubbed out. I want to say *he never deserved you*. I want to tell him that.

'Leave him be, Arthur.' May hisses it from the doorway. She's standing there with her hands on her hips giving me the look. 'What are you doing?'

I wave her away, 'He's sleeping. I'm not doing anything.'

'Imagine if he wakes up now, with your ugly mug hovering over him. He'll be traumatised for life.'

Stand up and my knees crack. Everything seizing up.

'Haven't you finished that cake yet?'

'Not quite.'

'What're you doing out here then? Get back in the kitchen, woman.'

She rolls her eyes. 'Ha, ha, very funny.'

I follow her into the hall, through to the doorway.

'Any mixture going?'

'Not yet. You need a shower.'

'Thanks for the advice.'

But she's right. I stink. The rain's seeped right in through the seams of the crappy waterproof. Wet patches on my shirt that could be sweat or water. There's no way of telling. I finished early – rushed through my round to get back and see him. Feel like I've been walking for a thousand years. The warmth is wearing off now. If I don't get dry soon I'll be chilled to the bone.

'Karen rang,' May says.

'How is she?'

'Angry mostly. But it won't last.'

'No sign of Ian?'

'Nothing. The police have been round.'

'Again?'

'One final search they said.'

'What the hell has that bastard been up to?'

'They won't tell her much. Still think she's hiding things.'

'Should I go over?'

'She said she wanted to be alone for a while.'

I rub my hand over my eyes. I should've done something. I don't know what I could've done.

'It'll be alright,' May says, 'we'll make sure they're both ok.'

'Thank goodness she never married him.'

She holds up a hand covered in flour or icing sugar and strokes her fingers across my forehead, touches the tip of my nose.

'Oh look,' she says, 'you've got a little something on your face.'

I run up the stairs because when my legs are stiff like this the only way is to push through it. Turn on the shower. The steam filling the bathroom, covering the mirror. One day, when Alex is older he's going to want to know about his dad. He's going to want to know why he buggered off. Who knows what we'll be able to tell him? Whatever we tell him he should know he was always a blessing to us. Scrub away the sweat and the ink and the grime of letterboxes and rusty gates and the stinking dogs who rub up against to me and sniff at the sour stains on the mailbag. Wash away the rain.

The day after Alex was born the sun was cracking flags. It was a relief to get inside. We waited for the lift in the hospital. May had a blue gift bag with a teddy in it – the bear with the red buttons and the pull cord that played a lullaby and broke before he was two because he asked for it so often. We could hear the lift coming down, the creaking, the warm rush of air.

'Alright?' I squeezed her arm and she just looked at me as if to say *Stop fussing, I'm fine.* I couldn't think what to talk about. I wanted to say *It smells just the same doesn't it?* I wanted to say *It feels as if it was yesterday.*

We stood inside, heard a man shouting 'hold on!' just as the doors were sliding shut, running forward, his foot wedged in the gap, arms pushing outwards against the force of the doors. May pressed the hold button and he fell in, pulling a helium balloon behind him. We made room. We smiled.

'Cheers,' he said, out of breath, 'if I'm late she'll kill me.'

He had a tracksuit on and trainers. His eyes were bloodshot. He ran his hand over the stubble on his head, back and forth like sandpaper on wood. He flooded the place with the smell of cheap aftershave. The balloon was wafting around in the space above out heads, like a plane with skywriting. *It's a boy!* reflecting it in all the mirrors, on the back of the doors, every-where. That feeling in my guts as the lift started upwards.

'Your first is it?' I said.

'Yep.'

'Let me guess. A little boy by any chance?'

'Yes!' he said, all excited, his eyes lighting up. He saw my face then, looked up at the balloon, laughed at himself.

May elbowed me in the side.

'Over nine pounds he is,' he held up a carrier bag, 'I've had to get the next size up in all the clothes. Chubby little bugger.'

'A good healthy weight,' May said.

'Tell that to the Missus.'

We laughed. But I was worried about May. I was worried about her seeing Alex. Karen had already told us about his hair when we rang. 'There's not much of it,' she said, 'but when the light catches you can really tell.' And he was so tiny, not much bigger than our little one when he – when we – and she'd held him then too, and smoothed the hair behind his ear, and I was worried it would all be too much.

We sat by the bed in the ward, and Karen was so proud of him and she lifted him into May's arms so gently and he was fast asleep, and I needn't have worried, because even asleep he was entirely himself, stretching like an old man after dinner, pursing his lips, forehead wrinkled like he was thinking deep thoughts. White, white skin with red patches as though they'd scrubbed him raw after he came out. Unmistakably alive.

'He's a little bobby dazzler,' I said and May smiled and held him as though she held newborn babies every day, and there was no sadness in her face, no tension at all.

'Where's Ian?' I said finally. Alex gripped one of my fingers inside his little hand. Karen wouldn't meet my eye.

'Probably gone to get a brew.'

The way she said it was off somehow, like there was more to it. I wanted to say more but Alex woke up and blinked, and his eyes were still dark, before the colour changed to grey. He shook his head from side to side and stared to cry. May lifted him onto her shoulder and he pushed at her with his hands, lifting his head up, searching and wailing.

'He's hungry, love,' May said.

'Oh right.' Karen glanced at me and sat up on the bed. May

pressed my foot with her foot. She needn't have bothered. I was already planning my escape. I stood up.

'I'll go and see where Ian's got to shall I? Could do with a brew myself.'

'Milk and two sugars,' May said.

Now the smell of cake wafting up from downstairs, my stomach rumbling like mad. I could murder a cup of tea. At the hospital it was all disinfectant and synthetic curtains, white tiles and the nurses rushing around with clipboards and drips. I couldn't shake the image of May holding him like that – so naturally. The sun coming in though the window behind her – like the stained glass window in the church when we finally got married, Mary and Jesus so peaceful and glowing, drawing me to them so I almost wanted to believe.

Time to get out. The ends of my fingers are wrinkled. Turn off the shower and rub myself dry and put on some clean clobber, warm from the radiator. There's no chance of any cake until Alex wakes up.

Ian was nowhere to be seen by the drinks machines. I traipsed up and down a few times and then got the lift back downstairs. Someone had left a newspaper on a bench in the reception. The *Times* from a day or two before, plastered with photos of the stadium disaster in Belgium. Juventus supporters and ambulance men dragging the bodies out of the stands. A disgrace from start to finish. I folded it and held it under my arm and stood outside and looked for Ian. Clouds of fag smoke and people in hospital gowns with their eyes closed against the sun, the sound of car doors slamming, a tall guy pushing an empty wheelchair and looking lost, the sound of kids laughing somewhere in the distance. I found him round the corner smoking a roll up, smoking and looking up to the sky. I said his name but he didn't hear, didn't notice me until I was right next to him, tapping him on the shoulder. He jumped.

'Jesus, Arthur! You scared the life out of me.'

'Sorry,' I said. 'How you doing? You look tired.'

But it was more than that. He looked edgy, wired somehow. He looked like he was just coming down.

'I don't think it's really sunk in yet – you know?'

'He's a little cracker.'

'Yeah.' He took a drag. His fingers were stained.

'Have you heard when you can take them home yet?'

'Tomorrow morning probably. Maybe today if the doctor comes round in time.'

'That's when the fun really starts.'

'And the hair,' he said, 'it's definitely, I mean – I never thought in a million years I'd produce a ginger kid.' He smiled but it was hollow. He shook his head, dropped the fag end and crushed it with his foot.

'Did Karen never tell you I used to have red hair? Well – auburn really.'

He looked at me properly for the first time.

'No shit.'

I laughed.

'It runs in May's family as well, you know. Sometimes skips a generation.'

'That explains it then.'

'I'm sure he'll survive.'

Ian laughed but it sounded forced. He started patting the pockets on his jeans as if to reassure himself everything was in place.

'I'm popping into the pub tonight,' he said, 'wet the baby's head and all that. You fancy it?'

I knew the place he meant. Rough round the edges, everybody drinking to get drunk. I wanted to say he should stay at home, lay off for a bit, sleep while he still could. I didn't.

'Early start tomorrow. I'm usually fast off by nine.'

'Don't know how you do it.'

'You get used to it. Let's go and get a brew shall we?'

He nodded but he looked like he wanted to run in the other direction. I steered him round towards the entrance and he kept shaking his head, hitting the side of it like he was trying to get water out of his ear after swimming. I pretended not to notice. I dropped the newspaper back on the bench on the way in. I didn't mention the football, even though I was dying to talk to someone about it all, the UEFA ban and the death toll and the shame of it. But I'd seen how he was at matches. I was scared of what he'd have to say. So we walked over to the lift in silence and I couldn't stop thinking about Joe Fagan, crying on the pitch in Belgium, not believing his own eyes, pleading with the fans and sounding like some bullies had ruined his birthday party: 'This is a football match,' he said, 'it's my last game as manager and you're spoiling it.'

It's all about Alex now. After tea we fill him full of cake and ice cream because that's what grandparents are for and we let him loose under the table, round our feet, playing with Karen's old toys. We sit there licking our fingers, trying to pick up the last few crumbs from the plates.

'I don't think he's coming back,' May says, 'not if he's in so much trouble.'

'Karen says they had a row.'

'There's more to it than that. He's taken everything. She came back from work and he'd completely cleared his stuff.'

'He was never a very hands-on father.'

'No. But still.'

Alex was pulling the plastic Fisher Price train, trying to re-couple a carriage that had tipped and come loose. Filling it too full of little uniform people with their plastic heads and moulded solid bodies.

'Billy said something once, at the match.' I said.

'What?'

'He said he saw Ian in the toilets with some dodgy-looking blokes all huddled together. There was money changing hands. They caught him staring and pinned him against the wall and then Ian recognized him and called them off, spoke to him nice as anything and told him to forget all about it.'

'You should've said something.'

'What good would that've done?'

'We could've warned Karen.'

'She wouldn't have listened.'

May starts to get up to clear the dishes, I reach out and hold her arm. She looks at me. She waits.

'What will we tell him, when he's older?' I say.

'That's up to Karen.'

'Yes – but you know what it's like, how hard it is without a dad, and what it's like to have questions.'

She goes stiff. We don't talk about this. It's off limits. Her mother burnt most of his things one day in one of her mad dos.

'I was older,' she says, 'he went off to fight. It's different.'

'But you still wanted to know the truth about the way he left, didn't you?'

She picks up the dishes.

'And I had people lining up to give me all the details,' she says, 'but the only person I really wanted to hear it from was him.'

She tucks Alex into Karen's old bed, and leaves the little lamp on so he won't get scared. She reads a story about a daddy-bear who can't find anywhere to sleep and I worry that he'll ask about Ian but he doesn't. By the end of it I'm yawning. I lean on the door. She's saying a prayer, getting ready to leave. I lie down next to him on the bed and she laughs and says 'You'll be asleep before him, Arthur,' and I wave her away. We put our heads together. He smells of May's perfume. I close my eyes and after a while he whispers in my ear: 'I want Mummy.' And I don't hear it at first because I'm already drifting but he says it again. It may be the first thing he's said to me all evening now I come to think of it and I don't know what to do.

'She's coming in the morning,' I say, 'just go to sleep now.'

But his face, which is right next to mine, so close I can feel every breath, crumples up, and he's crying silently at first and then wailing and saying her name over and over.

'Shhhh,' I say, and pat his arm and try to give him a toy to hold, but this is getting beyond me. I have to roll over, so stiff now I'm not sure I can even get off the bed. I roll over with a thud onto the carpet and push myself upright. I collide with May in the doorway.

'What did you do?'

'Nothing! He just started crying.'

She shoves me out the door and sighs as if to say she could've predicted this would happen, she could've predicted she'd be the one cleaning up my bloody mess.

'Get yourself to bed,' she says. One last order before she gives him all her attention. And I do. I stagger into the bedroom and fall down on top of the duvet and listen to her singing, *You are my sunshine, my only sunshine, you make me happy, when skies are grey.* For a minute I think of Ian holding Alex in the living room one Sunday afternoon, throwing him too high in the air and Karen behind him all worried but not wanting to interfere, and his little face all shocked and full of wonder.

I shuffle about and pull the duvet over me. I imagine Ian driving though the night – running away from Alex, running away from himself and even though he's a selfish bastard I feel a little bit sorry for him. Just a little. I think about the first time I'll take Alex to a match and how I'll keep him away from all the trouble. I'll keep him away from it for as long as I can. The music goes on: 'Strangers in the Night', 'Nature Boy', 'How Great Thou Art'. She doesn't remember half the words and she's never been renowned for her musical abilities and all the time I can hear the rain on the roof. The crying has stopped now and that song again, *I see the stars, I hear the rolling thunder.* I close my eyes and at this particular moment it may just be the loveliest sound I've ever heard.

1:30 pm

I don't know how they expect me to sing with my mouth full. These songs are good but they're not the one

And though we spoke of many things, many things, this he said to me —

Fancy hats and sugar on the vegetables. Sugar! The women check the plates. They add more potatoes when you're not looking. Their painted faces, all sparkle and glitter. They'd be better off going on the stage.

I don't want any more, thank you very much. I never wanted any in the first place.

The girl would understand if I could get her to   look. Not like the others. Her hair is   simple. She has a clean face. She doesn't grin at me like

angels we have heard on high   if there was a message she'd pass it on. If Ned was here she'd know.

Secrets are bad but sometimes there's no other way.

Dad sent me to the farm with the letter. The foxgloves tickled my legs. He said to put it under the bucket by the coal cellar. He said the postman had left it behind. I didn't tell Mum. 'She wouldn't like you going there, May,' he said.

The stamp was missing on the envelope.

18 May 1994

Alex

Billy won't stop singing. *Champio-nees, Champio-nees, away away away.* He's in the backseat drowning out the radio. Granddad stops at the traffic lights just before Sainsbury's and shakes his head.

'Don't get cocky Billy lad. We're already two–nil down.'

'But we can do it, Arthur. We're on our own turf now. Just watch us pulverise the bastards.'

I look out the window so he won't see me laughing. It's the sort of thing he usually saves for the Blackpool results. Hoping and hoping that they'll be relegated to division three, or that we'll go up to join them, so he can tell the donkey-lashers to their faces to shove the fucking tower up their arse. He's meant to reign it in around me, but things slip out. He can't help himself. I make my face serious, pretend I didn't hear. Turn back and stretch out my legs. We're earlier than usual but there are already fans everywhere. Five men wearing home shirts and jeans, crossing right in front of us even though the lights are green.

'Get a move on, lads,' Granddad says, but he doesn't beep the horn.

I try the handle on the glove compartment and it pops

open. The WD40 rolls out onto my foot and out of reach. He doesn't even notice. The car park is packed. He drives right round to the far corner and backs into a space like a pro.

And then we're walking up the hill to the stadium. It's hard to keep up. Billy is almost skipping. He looks like a wally. Like someone pretending to be a kid. I hope no one from school sees us.

'It's a long-shot, mate, that's all,' Granddad says, 'we'd need three goals. And that's only if they don't score.'

'But we can do it,' he looks at me for a second, 'Al agrees with me, don't you, Al?' he doesn't wait for an answer. 'We can get to Wembley. We can win it on aggregate. Those are the rules.'

He keeps saying that word. *Aggregate*. Like he's proud of it. Like he wants everyone to know that he knows what it means. I wish he didn't have to come. I wish he wouldn't call me Al. And then I feel bad for thinking it. Because I know what Nan would say. I've heard her arguing with Mum. *He's not a bad lad, just needs some looking after* and Mum saying *why does it always have to be you, though? He's always had a thing for me. It's creepy. And don't look at me like that. You can't deny he's a couple of sandwiches short of a picnic.*

Granddad manages to get us a spot by one of the blue railings on the Kop, right behind the goal and we lean there and just take it all in. The Town End already going mad with balloons and drums and newspaper confetti. Someone is throwing whole bog rolls out onto the pitch. The Torquay fans look puny, all hemmed into their bit of the stand, surrounded by fences. I can't hear them over our chants and the horns and the trumpet. Then it's the announcements. Birthdays and mascots, a reminder that it'll be the last game ever played on the plastic pitch. A cheer goes up.

'About bloody time,' Granddad says, clapping, 'about bloody time.'

I look down. The edges of the pitch look like they're coming loose. Like a faded carpet. The last team in the whole country to go back to grass. It's a joke. An embarrassment. But none of it really matters now. The teams are running out and it's all *come on you whi-ites*. Our lot looking smart in their plain tops and navy shorts. And the Torquay players in fussy yellow shirts with black stripes.

'Like fucking bumblebees,' someone shouts from behind us. And we're laughing and whistling while their names are read out. We're drowning them out one by one.

The drums start up as soon as the whistle blows for kick off. No one keeps possession for long. One of the Torquay players falls and rolls around on the plastic grass holding his knee and gurning with pretend pain. It starts from the other end of the stadium. *Soft southern bastard, he's just a soft southern bas-tard…* over and over. The medics run onto the pitch but he's up again before they can open their bags.

'Put your stretchers away!' Billy shouts, 'there's nothing wrong with him.'

And I'm watching the fans in the Town End. Never still. Always the loudest, the first to start the rudest chants. I imagine

Dad over there standing near the trumpeter and singing at the top of his voice. His face like it is in the photograph I found in a box Mum was getting ready to chuck out. I swiped it and hid it somewhere she'd never look. Slipped it into the middle of the Bible. Somewhere in the New Testament, between Jesus being born and resurrected. In the photo his eyes are red. He looks like he's about to punch whoever's holding the camera. I never let onto her that I had it. I asked Nan about him and she told me he was long gone and not coming back. 'He wasn't cut out for it,' she said once, 'he loved you but he just wasn't ready to be a father.' And then she ruffled my hair. I knew I shouldn't talk about it anymore.

The game starts up again but I can't concentrate. I can't help wondering what it would be like to bump into him. Maybe in the queue by the turnstiles or on the high street in town. He'd say *Look how big you're getting. Bloody hell, I wouldn't have recognised you.* And he'd crouch down and say *Mate, I'm sorry. I should never have left but look here* – all the different possible reasons he hadn't been in touch. Drafted into Special Forces and forbidden to contact family. Taken hostage by Russian spies, lying somewhere in a coma and only just recovering his memory.

And then everyone's going mad. Granddad punching the air. Strangers hugging each other. Billy screaming like a wild animal right next to my ear. I go on tiptoe to get a better look above the bobbing heads, people jumping in front of us.

'Straight off his head!' Billy says grabbing my arm, 'did you see it, Al? Play-offs here we come!'

I nod. I don't let on that I missed the whole thing. The players are hugging each other. And in the Town End they're pointing, rocking back and forth towards the away fans singing — *Who are ya? Who are ya? Who are ya?* Like a birdcall, getting louder until every voice in the world is united. As if it's all over. But it's not the end. We need another goal. Two more to really beat them. There's the whole match ahead and Granddad gripping onto the rail as if his life depends on it. I do the same. I hold on so tight that my hands start to hurt. I want it for him. I say a prayer with my eyes open. Because at church they say that God notices everything. Nothing is too small. If you have faith the size of a mustard seed then nothing is impossible. I watch them losing possession again and tell myself I have faith. Bigger than a mustard seed. Big enough to fill my whole body. I believe that they can win. I don't take my eye off the ball for a minute. *Please, please, please, bless them with strength. Bless them to win.* And the crowd start singing a hymn. Or close enough. *Oh how I want to be in that number, when the whites go marching in.*

It doesn't work. One of the bumblebees gets a clear shot. The look on his face as the ball goes in. Like even he can't believe his luck. He runs into the middle of the pitch and does a roly-poly. One of the reserve squad meets him on the sidelines for a quick high-five. The away fans are the ones making all the noise now. I try not to look, but I can't help it. A lad a few years younger than me on his dad's shoulders, laughing and waving a giant blow-up banana.

It's never simple. One step forward and another one back.

Shot after shot missing the mark. The excitement when they get a corner. The players grabbing shirts competing for headers, the other team taking too long to throw the ball back into play. My faith is gone now. I don't have any real power. The mountain is never going to move. And just as I think it someone kicks the ball to Moyesy and it's in. It's in. The noise is too much. When the half-time whistle blows the crowd are singing *I can't help falling in love with you* and Granddad joins in, clapping and stamping the rhythm out with his feet.

We queue up for meat pies and everyone's talking about it. Daring to hope.

'If they hadn't let that goal in,' Granddad says but he doesn't finish the sentence.

It's still a long shot really. Still one more goal before we even equalise. A group of men behind us are already drunk. Swaying all over, their voices too loud, pushing forward so that we all stumble and jam into each other.

'Calm it down, lads,' Granddad says. He has a way about him, somehow. He never gets people's backs up.

They stop pushing. One of them even says sorry. I can smell fried onions, hot chips and gravy. I look up at Granddad. His face. His full head of white hair, swept to the side, stuck down with so much gel that the wind doesn't stand a chance. I put my hand into the pocket of his coat. There's always some change jingling at the bottom. I feel for a pound coin, to test him, but he doesn't react. He doesn't try to stop me. I let it drop and take my hand away. He's distracted. Something's up with Billy. He's facing backwards, staring at the men behind us with his gob hanging open. He doesn't move when the queue shuffles forward.

'Billy, lad, stop gawping will yer?' Granddad forces him back round.

'It's him,' Billy says, and he's rocking forward and back on his heels. His face stretched out. His bottom lip trembling.

'Who?'

He's whispering now and Granddad pulls him close, stops him from turning round again. 'Him – Ian. Behind us.'

That name. I can't think. My ears are tingling with it.

'Shush, now. It's not,' Granddad looks at me and back to the group.

I play dumb. I glance around but my eyes won't focus. I've imagined seeing him here so many times. 'What's going on?'

'Nothing. Just Billy being daft. Do you want a pie or a burger?'

While he's ordering I risk it. I sneak a look. I can see who he means straight away. A tall lanky man, standing apart from the others, doing some sort of impression that has them in stiches. It's not him. He looks like the photo. But his eyes are different. The stubble is too dark on his chin.

Billy forgets all about it as soon as the match starts again, but I can't think about anything else. The look on his face when he thought it was my dad. I've never seen him so scared. Like he was going to piss himself. I want to know and I don't want to know. My stomach hurts. I wish I hadn't had the pie after all.

We score again. We equalise and Granddad squeezes my arm so hard it hurts. The noise dies down and he's muttering something under his breath. He's saying 'Don't get cocky, lads,' and I don't know if he means the fans or the players. I wish I was back at the house with Nan. I've heard Mum whispering to her about me. Afraid I'm too quiet. Afraid there's something wrong. And Nan says I'm special and different and it's nothing that a bit of time and cake won't fix. I want to be in the chair by the bookcase. Close my eyes and picture an oak leaf. *Sinuate, undulate, wavy.* The furry underside of a mulberry leaf. The bark of a London Plane tree patterned like camo. It's going dark now and the wind is cold. The floodlights too bright. The hairs on my arm are standing up. The match is going on and on. They're starting to get ready for extra time. Over on the Town End they're already singing about Wembley.

'Don't count your chickens,' Granddad says and Torquay's keeper takes a goal kick to the sound of *youuuuuu're shit!* rising up in time with the ball.

I don't pray. I don't even try to have faith. But the miracle happens anyway. Another goal in extra time. They manage to hold them off until the final whistle blows. Everyone starts pushing forward. We stay leaning on the railing letting them knock us on their way past.

'I told you,' Billy says, 'didn't I tell you they'd do it?'

'You did,' Granddad says patting him hard on the back, 'you bloody did.' His voice is croaky from shouting. For a minute I think he might even cry.

People are jumping over railings now, invading the pitch. Hundreds of them legging it past the stewards until it's hard to see any green.

'Remember this moment, lad,' Granddad says, 'this is a piece of history.'

I look around and try to make my brain soak it in. Try to feel what he feels. The noise of it. The singing. Some of the players have been lifted into the air. The whole pitch is a sea of white. Except in the corner by the goal. I squint down, lean forward to get a better look. There's a young lad down there on his own. He's in a black jacket, bending over. He pulls an orange carrier bag out of his pocket and starts filling it with something. And then I realise. It's the pitch. Strips of green plastic. He must have a knife or some scissors with him. He's cutting and peeling. Slipping square after square into the bag to take home or sell or God knows what.

'We're off to Wembley, Al,' Billy says and slaps me on the back too hard.

'Tired, are you, lad?'

I nod, and we head towards the exit. I look back but the boy is gone.

We walk beside the other fans and everyone is laughing and shouting. I catch a glimpse of a yellow shirt. The away fans being herded onto a coach, surrounded by stewards and police. They don't look any of us in the eye. *You're not singing anymore*, someone shouts in their direction and a whole choir of voices joins in. *You're not sing-ing any-more*. I walk with my head down. Granddad roughs up my hair and checks to make sure I'm ok every time we cross the road. Billy is singing again. I want to tell him to shut his bloody pie-hole, but it's no use. The sound of all the horns beeping, people hanging white and blue scarves out their car windows and sticking their heads through sun roofs. It'll be all anyone's talking about at school. I try to picture the crappy green plastic being pulled up, the soil uncovered and dug over, planted with perfect grass ready for the new season but I can't imagine being back here to see it. I can't really imagine coming back here at all.

2:55 pm

The birds go tap, tap, tap, but I never learned Morse
code. I used to know
  things
Ostrich   lapwing   heron   tern.   None of them fit.
These
                    birds. All they want to do is get inside.

There's no green, not here, not for miles. The doors are
locked. I can't feed the birds in these shoes. These shoes are
soft. They
  bend too far

this seat is wet.
      my legs all fizzy
            if they knew the seat was wet they'd send the
birds away. And then I'll never find him
                        and

4 February 1997

Afsana

The air stings. I pull my scarf up over my mouth. The sky is blue, but winter blue. Sharp and mean. Not a single cloud. I lock the door and walk away from the flat, along the gravel by the hundred-year-old houses. The bay windows, and special parking permits, sitting right at the top of the hill so they can look down on everyone else. I follow their gaze. Down to the river, the green bowl of the park, the bandstand and the gatehouse and the Japanese garden. Dog walkers and people training for charity fun-runs and the man on the bench with his head in his hands like he's just heard some terrible news.

Ewan has a lot time for the Victorians. They had vision, a sense of the future. They planted the avenue of trees by the river knowing full well they wouldn't live to see it mature. 'There's something impressive about that isn't there?' he said once, ' leaving a legacy for the next generation, building something that'll last for hundreds of years after you're gone.' We were in the flat one Saturday, taking a break from revision. Drinking coffee. I nodded. I was thinking about Baba, and the surah about rewards after death. So many ways to cement your place in paradise. Building a mosque, planting a date palm, leaving behind a righteous child who'll pray for you after you've gone.

'Come with me,' he said. He seemed excited, eager like he got sometimes when he was talking about something he loved. I followed him across the room and he opened the door to the bedroom. I hesitated. I didn't want him to know what I was thinking. So I went in. Everything was too neat. Just an alarm clock on the bedside table. The wardrobe and drawers shut flush. The beige carpet newly hoovered. Like a hotel, or at least like I imagined a hotel to be. He stood by the window and pulled the blinds up. No dust on the sill. The light coming in, shining on the white walls.

'Look,' he said. And I did. I stood right next to him so our arms were almost touching. This same view, just cut up a bit by the window frames, blocked by the roofs of all the posher houses. The trees were green that day. There were tulips in the borders and the river wasn't quite as high.

'Designed to last,' he said and I thought about Baba talking to his friends about the British. The English Viscount who carved up their country by drawing a pencil line on an out-of-date map. Ewan looked at me, grinning. He said, 'so what do you think of my back garden?'

We never went to the park to work. Not even when it was hot and full of students lying on their bellies, falling asleep into their textbooks. Sometimes we could hear children shouting through the window. He must've known it was a risk for me to come over on the train every weekend but he never mentioned it. We both pretended it was normal. He never asked me what lies I had to tell. There was always a chance of bumping into a friend of a friend of a wife of a second cousin once removed. Sometimes between the train station and the flat I saw girls with patterned headscarves, jeans under dresses, fitted jackets and lipstick. I had to stop and make sure it wasn't Amina. I had to catch my breath. That summer her favourite hijab was dark grey threaded with silver. She didn't argue when Dadi laid the law down. She was too practical for that. She embraced it as another styling opportunity.

I walk down the crumbling steps and across to the old tram bridge. Soon Ewan will be home from work. The flat will be dark. Nothing cooking. No note to say where I am. It's getting to be a habit. The river winding out of sight on either side. The sun going down on the water and the fields. It doesn't feel like you're within spitting distance of the town centre. It feels like you could just keep walking into the country and never come back.

There's a woman coming across the bridge with a pram and a toddler in tow. The little boy's carrying a big stick. He hangs back, looking through the metal bars at the water and the little pockets of ice, and the ducks making noise and flapping at each other. Threatening to fly. She's way ahead of him now, passing me and onto the path and round the corner. I wonder how long until she notices he's not following. He leans into the railings, sits down on the tarmac. His feet and hands slip through the bars and his puffy coat is all flattened in places, like a belt pulled too tight, or an elastic band snapped tight over fat rolls. He swings his legs from side to side in the air above the river. His scarf is loose and dangling. It could easily fall off. It would fall, like a ribbon into the water. I look back towards the park. She's stopped, finally. She turns around to look for him.

'Oi! Get 'ere now!' Her voice echoes. It sends the ducks into a frenzy. 'Don't make me come over there,' she says. 'Here. Now.'

It cuts through everything. He gets up and walks slowly. He runs the stick across the railings and I can feel the rhythm of it in my fingers. His mouth is stained red at the sides with juice. It makes him look like he's smiling, but he isn't. He lets go of the railings and walks around me as if I don't exist. His scarf is dragging on the ground now. She waits until he's right in front of her, then bends over, pulls the scarf away and throws it back into his face. Right back. Like a whip. I look away. I imagine him shutting his eyes against the slap of the tassels.

'Put. It. Round. Your. Fuckin'. Neck.'

They head down the hill towards the pavilion and I can't help thinking about the lectures from Dadi. So many. They all merged into one after a while. The honour of raising righteous daughters. The honour that Baba deserves.

'These girls here love dunyah more than honour,' she said one dinnertime when Amina was waiting to escape, to go out to the cinema with friends. 'They think of their own desires and nothing else. They show everything they have, they give for free to anybody and because of that what are they worth?'

'Nothing,' Amina said, and I looked at her to see if she was being serious or just playing along. I couldn't tell.

Breathe out and send my breath over the railings. I can still hear the pram wheels on the gravel. That poor boy. He didn't seem fazed. He's probably been through worse. I try to think through the argument with Ewan, the latest one, to understand how I got from there to here. I left the newspaper open at the jobs page. That was the first mistake. He was looking at it in the kitchen first thing when I came out of the bedroom. Almost dressed for the commute, pushing the wide end of his yellow tie through the loop, pulling it tight. I brushed past him and picked the kettle up to fill it, turned the tap off, put the kettle back on its stand, flipped the on switch.

'So you want to be a care assistant now?'

'What?'

'A care assistant.'

He picked up the paper and shoved it under my nose. I'd circled the advert in a moment of boredom the day before. A moment when the thought of another shift in the shop was so depressing anything new seemed possible.

I shrugged. It was too early. I wanted to say *Let me get a cup of coffee, Ewan, let me do that at least.*

'You've never worked in care.'

I closed my eyes, pressed them shut with my fingers until all I could see were coloured spots and patterns like chess-boards and the tiles in the big book of Islamic architecture Baba hardly ever let me get down off the shelf. The kettle started to hiss.

'I've worked with people.'

'You sell shoes. I mean, granted – to the same sort of

clientele,' he laughed, 'but come on, Sana – it hardly counts as experience.'

The way he said it. I felt all protective suddenly, of the shop and the ugly sandals and slippers with ergonomic insoles, and all the people who just wanted to be comfortable. The loose skin on their feet and the bunions and big dark veins. I grabbed the paper, held it right against my face, as if that would help the words to crawl into my brain, and come out perfectly.

'It says here... experience preferred... but not essential as full training will be given.'

He grabbed it back. 'They'll treat you like crap, Sana. Have you seen the hours? This is a vocation, not something you just wake up one day and decide to do.'

'Why don't you just say that you think I'm incapable?'

'*In*capable you mean? And no I don't think that. We've been through this. If you really want a change I can help you with the exams. I can enter you as an independent candidate. Once you have the English and Maths, there'll be so many more options to look at.'

I shook my head. Bloody tears. Just the thought of it. The test booklets and the clock ticking and the questions blurring into one. Ewan repeating all the rules. *Don't spend too long on one section. Always check how many points it's worth. Remember to put a line through your working out. Plan your answers. Don't panic, just concentrate and show that you've understood. Make sure you've read the question properly.*

'You can't just give up, Sana!'

'I'm not giving up. I'm looking into other possibilities.'

'Fine.' He put his cereal bowl into the sink so carefully it didn't make a sound. He started to walk to the door, picked up his bag and coat then doubled back.

'Just don't expect me to help with the application.'

'I won't.'

'And don't come running to me in a few months complaining that you'd rather be measuring their feet again, instead of wiping their arses.'

The final word. He slammed the door. The kettle boiled as if on cue. I laughed until it wasn't laughter. Until there were tears and snot and I tried to sip the coffee but I couldn't, because of the aftershocks, the sobs that made me feel like I was five again and made me miss Mum more than I'd ever missed her before. Baba always said I was like her. Quiet and modest. But quietness doesn't always go with obedience. Quiet people are better at hiding things. I wondered if she would've taken my phone calls, come to visit even. Sometimes I dare to imagine she would've wished me well. I think of her muttering the only prayer she knew by heart. Calling down protection. Banishing illness. I want to ask her to tell me how she met Baba again. The local council planning section. He asked her to deal with all his applications because she was so efficient. Their wedding was nothing like in the films. A quiet meeting with the imam and a quick service in the registry office. She had no representatives. There was no one to give permission. There's a blurred photo of them standing outside the town hall. Her hair isn't covered, she's wearing a long flowery dress. Her face is side-on because she's looking at Baba. I wonder if they mocked up something more traditional to send to Dadi, to soften the blow. I wonder if she was ever really converted, which bits of it she actually believed. The way she's looking at him in that photo, the answer's not really that complicated. She believed in him.

Sometimes I dream that she's trying to find me but she can't, because I'm not on the straight path that leads to Jannah, I've sacrificed it all and there's nothing left but ashes and dust.

So I walk because it's the only thing left to do. If I walk long enough maybe I can let go of this feeling and be ready to make peace. To stop being so selfish. It's almost dark. Walk by the old-fashioned lamps. Yellow light making everything feel like history. Under the railway bridge. Always the drips, even if it hasn't rained for days. Graffiti: *Carli W takes it up the arse*. A giant penis in white paint. I push on to the houses. Past the pub. Families going in to eat. Lights in the windows. It's safer here after dark. Safer and lonelier at the same time.

The Saturday after the exams there was no real reason to get the train to Ewan's. He'd told me I was welcome, that we could celebrate, go over some of the questions, whatever I wanted. So I went anyway. I left earlier than usual. I didn't tell anyone I was going. I didn't repeat the lie about revising in the library with Nafisa. They wouldn't have believed it anyway. There were boxes stacked in the hall. No photographs on the walls. I should've stayed at home to help pack, but the thought of not being with him – of not even getting to say thank you and goodbye was too much.

When he opened the door he was smiling. He was wearing denim shorts and a checked shirt. He looked like he was going to the beach.

'What's wrong?' he said as soon as he saw my face, 'come in and sit down. For God's sake – what on earth's the matter?'

He put his hands on my shoulders and guided me to the sofa. I couldn't speak. I kept shaking my head to clear it. Then he was next to me. His arm was around me.

'The exams can't have gone that badly, surely, Sana.'

I wanted to tell him they had. They'd been a total disaster. But that wasn't why I was crying.

'I'm moving,' I said finally.

'Oh.' He sat up. 'Where?'

'Leicester.'

'That's a bit sudden.'

'The house is finished. It's a private sale. I was hoping we'd stay close by, but my Dad found a new project over there, so…'

'When are you going?'

'A week or two.'

'That's quite a way. What about college?'

All the applications he'd helped me with. With my grades they'd probably be worthless anyway. I shrugged. He stood up.

'We need a coffee.'

He went into the kitchen and I sat there thinking I should've stayed at home. What exactly did I expect him to do? This was how he was going to remember me. Pathetic. I wiped my eyes on my sleeve. I waited for him, but I knew that after the coffee all that was really left was to go home and face Dadi. Stand back while she mapped out my future. *Achieving in school is not for everyone, Sana.* Opening those brown envelopes. The photos of nice young Pakistani men with big side partings and serious faces. Like they've been told not to smile. Like Victorians.

He put the mugs on the coffee table and sat down. He turned towards me. I thought he was going to tell me he was sorry, wish me luck, all that politeness. He didn't. He swallowed. He looked nervous.

'You mentioned once that you hadn't always worn the headscarf.'

I was confused. It wasn't what I was expecting. I put my hands to my head.

'What changed?' he said.

'Things got difficult at home. It's easier like this.'

He looked at me then, right at me, not like before. It wasn't kindness. I should've lowered my eyes but I couldn't. He touched the side of my face.

'Take it off,' he said.

And I did.

*

My ears throbbing with the cold. Walking home in a big circle. He'll be there now, waiting, ready to give me a lecture. Past the school, all shut up and dark. But there are lights from the Hindu temple, the big white canopy gleaming like carved ivory, the dome rising up. The front doors are open. A banner for blood donation inviting people in. They do it here regularly. I've seen the posters, made a mental note to come down. But I never have, and now here I am by accident. Maybe it was fated.

There's a small queue at the reception desk and a waiting area with plastic chairs like we used to use in school assemblies. A special area for tea and biscuits. Portable screens and trolley beds and nurses and people lying on their backs attached to plastic tubes, squeezing their hands into fists, out and in, out and in, waiting for their lifeblood to drain out and be stored like magic.

I wait, and take it all in. The room is disappointing, like a school gym. It smells of spices, like our house always did after Dadi cooked. We'd only notice it when we'd been away – coming in from school or Mosque. I was expecting statues and offerings. The blue god with all the arms. Gold leaf and altars and embroidered fabric. Women dressed ready for a Bollywood dance routine.

'Do you have an appointment?'

'No.'

The reception nurse smiles at me. 'Have you donated before?'

'It's my first time.'

'No problem. We should be able to fit you in. Just fill this out and we'll find a space for you.'

She hands me a clipboard and a pen and points to the chairs behind me. One look at the form and I want to run. I want to turn and walk back out the door. The words are crammed together. So many questions. Nobody here to help me with spelling. I need to stop and calm down. It's not an essay. It's only ticking boxes. I don't know anyone who gives blood. No one ever said it was forbidden but it was a grey area, a kind of violation of the body. Who knew where your blood would end up? Too many question marks. It was better to be safe.

I breathe in and look around. All sorts of people. It's like someone's staged it for a leaflet, as an advert for diversity. A black man with a Rasta hat, a woman in a sari, a hard-looking bloke wearing overalls, the token male nurse. It's like heaven. Good people who come out on a cold afternoon to be stuck with a needle and ask nothing in return.

Concentrate on the words and don't chew the pen. You don't know where it's been. I can do this. I can. I want to be here. At this moment there's nowhere else I'd rather be. And Ewan's face when I tell him, when I get back to the flat later. He won't believe me. I'll show him the mark on my arm as proof. Shake the pen and scribble on a scrap of paper to check that it's working. It'll almost be worth it just for that.

3:10 pm

This is not a hospital.

    Think, May, think.

    Not a hospital, not a holiday, not a hotel, not a school, not *home*. This is nowhere.   These people aren't

    helpful

    they don't want me opening the doors –

No, thank you. I don't need any help from you. I don't want to listen to this music.

    They say he wandered very far, very far, over land and sea – but he's not here now

and these people are not my people.

1 April 2006

Karen

It takes me a while to spot her. The TV is blaring and they all sit in mis-matched armchairs and stare and rock and look, some of them, like they're going to dissolve. She's half asleep. Peaceful, almost. But thinner than last week. Her collarbones stick out too much. Her blouse is starting to hang loose across the chest.

I pull up a chair and sit opposite her, knee to knee. She sees me eventually. Her eyes flutter. She smiles. Like when Alex was little and he'd wake up from a nap with a face full of love.

'Finally,' she says, sitting up a little, 'have they sent you with my medicine?'

It must be the uniform or the way I've got my hair scraped back. 'No. It's me Mum, it's Karen.'

She narrows her eyes and looks away, out of the window at the plastic pots full of mini daffodils all starting to go brown and crispy at the edges.

'You never come to see me,' she says, 'and your lips are too bright.'

'I was here last week.'

'*And* they put sugar on the vegetables.'

'Yes, I know.'

'Sugar,' she whispers, leaning forward, 'on the vegetables. Like they're trying to fatten me up.'

'Well, you could do with putting on some weight. I might have a word.'

She rubs her hands together. Dry and chapped. She has that look on her face. Just like old times. Like when she saw me in the bus shelter with Simon Williams. Like when she found the packet of pills in my drawer.

'Your lips,' she says, pointing.

I should've known better than to wear the bloody lipstick. I try to blot it on the back of my hand, but it's a new long-wear formula. The colour's going nowhere.

'If you're looking for a man around here you'll be disappointed.'

'I'm not looking for a man.'

She keeps doing that thing with her hands. The noise it makes. It drives me mad. If she doesn't stop it she'll rub the skin right off. I reach out to hold them still and she jumps like I've given her an electric shock.

'Don't!' she says, 'you're always trying to meddle in my affairs.'

'Your hands are sore.'

She folds her arms and leans back. 'There's nothing whatsoever the matter with them and I don't need any help, thank you very much.'

'Ok!'

'And if you're looking for a man you won't find one around here. Not one with all his faculties at any rate.'

'I think you've made your point now, Mum.'

'Your body's a temple not a colouring book.'

'For God's sake!'

'I don't like that kind of language.' She's shifting in her seat now, looking around for someone to back her up, or a way to escape. I need to change the subject but I can't think of anything to say. I want to tell her all about Alex. I want to say, *That grandson of yours is messing up his life.* But who knows what she remembers? Knowing my luck it'd only make things worse.

There's an old episode of Top of the Pops on the TV. The Bay City Rollers jiggling about on stage with their bare chests and stupid half-mast flares. *Bye, bye baby, baby bye, bye.* The man in the next chair starts to groan and swear. The care assistant seems to materialise out of nowhere. The pretty one. Pretty and foreign-looking. She helps the man to stand up and walks with him over to the door. She has a nice way about her. Not like some of the others. She touches Mum's shoulder as she walks past and the way Mum looks up at her. Kindness and trust. Mum leans back in the chair and starts humming something with her eyes closed. Like she's trying to imagine me away.

'Tell me about Ned,' I say, just on the off chance.

She stops humming. She opens her eyes. She says, 'I don't think I'm allowed to talk about it.'

'You're allowed.'

She shakes her head. She starts to rub her hands again and

look in every direction but at me. 'He won't be able to find me here,' she says, 'even if he was looking he'd never know where I was. And I've got nothing to give him if he comes.' She holds her hands out then tries to push herself up out of the chair. It's no use. Her wrists are so thin. Her arms shaking with the effort. 'Look at this!' she says. 'Look at what you've done to me!'

'Calm down, Mum. It's alright.'

'It's not. You put me here to hide me away.'

'That's not –'

'I think you're very rude and your lips are too bright.'

She starts humming again. It's familiar. Slow and sad. Words scattered in here and there. *Very far, very far, over land and sea.* I can't place it.

'That's it then is it?' I say, 'conversation over?'

'If you don't mind there's somewhere I have to be at three-fifteen.'

'Is there? Where's that then? An urgent appointment with the commode? An especially good episode of Antiques-fucking-Roadshow?' I say it under my breath but she glares at me. There's nothing at all wrong with her hearing.

I go to sign out and my hands are shaking. The corridor is soupy with chemicals. The smell of meat and over-boiled vegetables. Someone's chewed the end of the pen by reception. Teeth marks in the cheap plastic. The door buzzes and clicks.

When I get home it's quarter to seven. The porch is full of

takeaway leaflets, money-off supermarket vouchers and junk mail. Saturday night. I can't bear to go in. Alex is already at work. Holed up in the pub kitchen, scraping gravy off the plates, stacking beer glasses in the big dishwasher. I'm past hunger. My toenails feel like they've been pushed too far into my skin. I could curl up on the sofa and let the night wash over me, wait for Alex to get in. He wouldn't thank me for it.

Something has to change. I put my bag down on the bottom step and lean against the banister. The primary school photo of Alex is wonky again. He does it on purpose. He used to turn it to the wall if Lorna was coming over. Embarrassed by the way his hair clashed with his maroon jumper. His gappy-toothed smile. I straighten it and stand back. The ticking of the boiler firing up. The hum of the fridge. Outside there's a siren getting louder and then fading away. There's no reason to waste another weekend. There's nothing here to stay for. I think of the gang from work, out for their usual weekend drinks. There's always room for one more.

On the bus into town. The driver is too hard on the brakes and I can feel the nausea starting. Root in my bag for an extra-strong mint. The rush of it, scouring out the inside of my head, pushing any other taste away. The seats are still ingrained with fag smoke even though smoking's been banned for years. There are lights on in all the houses. All those perfect families sitting around their dinner tables eating second helpings of steamed vegetables, discussing sports tournaments and out-standing school reports.

One of the bouncers salutes me as I walk into the club. I smile at him but he's not familiar. It's been years. He's just being friendly. For a minute the colours are blinding, glittering spots of light making everyone look golden and manic. The queue for the bar is five people deep. I can't see anyone from work. Stand on tiptoes and try to get a good view of the seats by the dance floor. Somebody pushes from behind. *Sorry, love.* It's all beer froth and sequins. I don't recognise the music and the bass is too loud. Hemmed in by bare arms, and shoulder blades. A fruity perfume I recognise from trying the tester at work. And the customer who turned her nose up when I tried to recommend it. *Do some people actually like this?* She said. *Do some women actually want to smell edible?*

And then Gary's hand is on my arm. I might have known it would be Gary. He's saying something, but I can't make it out.

'What?'

'I can't believe you actually made it!'

'Where are the others?'

'Come on,' he says, 'I saw you from the bar. I got you a rum and coke.'

He leads me around the dance floor to a dim corner, the edge of a long curved purple sofa near the toilets. It's almost full. There's barely enough room for two. A line of empty beer glasses on the table.

'Where are the others?'

Gary shrugs and waves towards the dancefloor. 'Last time I saw Donna she was admiring some Rugby players by the bar.'

The group of girls next to us stand up and push past in unison. They head towards the toilets together. One of them goes right over on her heel and falls against the wall. The others stand and laugh.

'I'm gonna piss myself!' she says sliding to the floor, 'fucking bitches.' But she's laughing too. One of her friends bends over to help her up.

Gary shakes his head. 'Mike and Jonsey are here somewhere. Half-way to shit-faced last time I checked.'

'I hope Mike's looking after him.' I can't imagine Jonsey drunk. He's so timid. He doesn't seem old enough to be in a place like this.

Gary shrugs. He leans in closer. Always too eager. Right up in my personal space.

'Have you heard the news?' he says. But I can't concentrate. I can't see anything but his receding hairline and greasy skin. Spots on his neck. His forehead shining under the lights. And all I can think is how am I back here? How come I never got out of this shit-hole when I had the chance?

'Sorry? What?'

'The news,' he says, louder this time. 'They've gone and sold Blackpool tower off for scrap.'

I don't know what to make of it. For a minute I think I must have misheard. He's waiting for my reaction.

'Really?' I say.

'Scout's honour. Lancashire County Council signed the deeds this morning.'

I take a sip of my drink and try to make sense of it. He's

grinning at me like a maniac. Like he's waiting for something. The truth is I don't really give a shit. They can melt it down and send it to the moon for all I care. There'd be a big crowd of tourists if they were really skint enough to do it – scratching their arses and taking photos, sucking sugar dummies and sticks of Blackpool rock. The creaking metal, and all the bolts wrenched out. The brown sea behind them. Full of God-knows-what.

'April fools,' he says, poking my leg to get my attention.

'Oh God, Gary. How many times?' Mike is back from the bar standing over us with a pint in one hand and a shot glass in the other. 'Do us all a favour and find some new material.'

Gary's smile fades.

'Oh, right,' I say, I'd forgotten about the date. 'Right. You really had me going there for a minute.'

They argue after that. I shuffle along so Mike can sit down. They push and jab at each other like lads on the playground. And then talk about football and the new sales targets and how useless the security guard is at work. I join in every now and then. Nod in the right places. But I'm thinking about Ian. I can't help it. That night we met. The same drink. The first year we lived together when he was building the business up. Storing the stock in the spare room. And me doing the books in the evenings. He was all gung-ho and high on ambition. If he could've been paid just for talking about it we would've been millionaires. I'd get in after work and there'd be no sign of him. Walking through the flat calling his name and I'd feel something on the back of my neck and there he was, creeping behind me with the severed plastic arm from one of the shop dummies. Or another time it was the shape of someone in our bed and him hiding in the wardrobe, waiting for me to lift the covers. He got a kick out of it, out of scaring me shitless and then making up for it after. Falling onto the bed together and the sound of him pushing the naked dummy onto the floor.

'You'll give me nightmares, you daft bastard.'

He was kissing my neck, then, fumbling one-handed with my bra strap. Him still laughing and me trying to remember if I'd taken my pill.

'Please tell me that's not the only thing you've been doing today.'

'Shhhh,' he said, 'shhhh,' and I wanted to kiss him and kill him in the exact same moment.

'You're not Jeremy fucking Beadle, you know.'

'Let's get out of here,' Gary says, and it's the first piece of sense I've heard from him all night.

Mike knows somewhere round the corner with 80s music and cocktails so we rescue Donna from the bar and head across the square.

'I deserve better,' she keeps saying to anyone who'll listen, 'I'm not just a piece of meat.'

'You're beautiful,' Mike says, 'You're an absolute catch. Now lean on my arm and shut the fuck up.'

Gary is singing Electric Dreams. He takes me in a ballroom hold and I'm not drunk enough yet but I can't be bothered to fight it. We trot across the road. All those dance classes in the church hall. I knew they'd come in handy one day. His hand too tight across my back. But he can hold a tune. I'll give him that. *We'll always be together*, he sings, *however far it seems*, and Mike is on backing vocals and Donna is laughing and my throat is dry. I need something sweet to keep me going.

'It's round this corner,' Mike says.

Gary stops dancing, and starts walking, but doesn't let go of my arm.

'Wait,' he says, stopping in his tracks. Donna bumps into me on the other side. 'Where the hell is Jonesy?'

We all look around but he's not behind us. He's nowhere near.

'I haven't seen him all night.'

'You lost him?' Donna says, 'you just left him there?'

Mike starts laughing so hard he's bent over with it.

Gary shrugs. 'I'm not his bloody father.'

'You're old enough,' Donna says.

'Says you, Mrs Mutton.'

She comes forward to slap him but trips on a loose paving stone and slams against me.

'Ow!'

'I'm sorry,' she says, and her words are slurred, one strap falling down across her shoulder, 'but he's a bastard.'

'Everyone just calm down,' Mike says. 'He probably just found someone he knew and buggered off like usual.'

'You better hope so,' Donna said, 'or it'll be on your head.'

I try to picture Jonsey in detail. His scruffy hair dyed a

couple of shades too dark for his skin. The way he lets it hang over one eye. The quietness, the way he blushes when he's put on the spot. He's not really cut out for customer service. I can't imagine him alone in the club.

'Stop over-reacting,' Gary says. 'He'll be reet. He'll have gone somewhere more suited to his tastes.'

'What do you mean?' Donna says.

'Oh come on,' Gary says, looking to Mike for support, 'I can't be the only one who thinks it?'

'What?' I say, but I know what he's getting at. It's dawning on me and I can't believe it's never occurred to me before.

Gary rolls his eyes. 'It's obvious isn't it? His best friends are all girls but he never has a girlfriend. He wears eyeliner. Do I need go on?'

'Yes,' Donna says.

'Ok then. He's dancing at the other end of the ballroom. Batting for the other team. Packing fudge for a living. Is that clear enough?'

I pull my arm away from him. I feel sick.

'Oh come on!' he says, 'just because I say what everyone else is thinking!'

'I'm going back,' I say and turn and start walking.

'Oh, come on!' Gary says, 'he's a big boy!'

Donna stumbles after me. 'He'll be long gone by now,' she says, 'don't leave me with them.'

'I can't stay.'

'You coming, Donna?' Gary shouts.

She shrugs and lets me go.

I can't face going back to the club. And it's not Jonsey I'm thinking about. It's Alex. A fucking light bulb throbbing right above my head. His whole life, everything has been pointing to this and I just didn't want to see. I get into a taxi and try to block out the music from the radio. Everything becoming clear. The way he was with Lorna. The way he hides himself away. Never quite fitting in. We stop at the lights. There's a billboard at the junction by the prison. Personal finance, maybe or life insurance. A girl wearing a graduation gown, standing next to her parents, her hat in mid-air. They're all looking up at it and smiling as though it's the proudest day of their lives. It's like someone planted it here just for me, just to rub salt in the wound. *Look at what you could have won.* I feel sick. I'll have to ask him about it. I'll have to shake all the secrets out of him. I root in my bag for another mint. Catch my wrist on the edge of a tube of hand cream. Mum's hands. I could have gone back and sorted them for her. I could've asked the girl to do it for me.

It's too late now. It's all too late. The lights are turning again, amber to green. One last look before we turn left. The girl's teeth are too perfect. Her parents look like ageing catalogue models. I know it's staged. I know it's only marketing. But oh God, I want it to be real. That's all. I just want it to be possible.

4:00 pm

Leave me with the light   I'm trying to see.   I'm trying to remember

      yellow leaves
      blue buttons
      bottletops
      the bird's egg with the crack
      the birds tapping on the glass   and

    Dad. There – by the window   if I go nearer he'll melt. Can't look, got to look. He's here to give me a sign.

A little shy,   and sad of eye   but very wise   was he.

    He isn't sad anymore. He doesn't need to say sorry He's with the birds. They're all trying to tell me. I'm ready. Oh! I've been ready for ever so long.

    He's not in the water now. The boy is safe. The rivers shall not overflow thee.

    He doesn't need to come any closer. He was never really gone.

I want to touch his hand but my legs are too damp.

I can't get any closer. But the sky is so clear.
And the light. I knew it! He's taken up!

24 July 1996

Arthur

Every breath is full of knives. Every breath brings stars and paisley patterns and the terror. I can't stand it. Cold hands – so cold – they might as well be the devil, moving me about, twisting the blades. *Arthur*, she says. But I'm so full of holes. So cold my hairs stand up and they hang me from the ceiling by the hairs on my arms, my chest, my legs. Pulling skin. Those hands – the buggering bloody piss-pot fuckers. Pulling at me, pressing all the bruises, punching again and again, straight in the bladder.

And then the peace. As sudden as rain, the peace floods in. Floating back down to the bed. The softness, the lifting. I love the hands that do this. So sacred I don't even open my eyes. They're sealed. The kindness is everywhere.

And I can go to the Field Day after all. May behind the tea stall. The dirty canvas of the tent going dap-dap-dap in the rain and the crowd of people and someone running, knocking over the teacup and the bounce of the china on the soggy ground and my mates saying 'Come on Arthur, it's all bobbins, there's nowt 'ere'. May behind the trestle table talking to her mother, frowning, arms folded and a space opening up. Walking over to pick up the cup and her legs under the table, her legs in stockings, and the wind catching her skirt. Banging my head on the table and her laugh, her eyebrows. She takes the cup and her fingers – her fingers! But the music is wrong, the music is always wrong, and the voices are from somewhere else. My mouth as dry as sand. There are hands on me and the warmth again, the relief, the lifting.

I want to stay in the tent. I've seen her in the Post Office, but this is different. There's no reason for me to stay in the tent. 'Cup of tea?' she says and her smile. Like she can see right through me, like she's hiding a whole different world behind the beautiful mask of her face. She'll be able to tell me anything at all. The universe is in there, the secrets, the meaning of everything. I'm see-through now, can feel myself evaporating in front of her like the steam from the big metal teapot. She could reach out and run her fingers through me and I'd be real again, solid and mangled like melted butter gone hard. That's how it feels, that's how it is. And I say 'No sugar' even though I like it sweet and her dress is blue and her breasts – her breasts – I shouldn't think about her breasts. Later in the bus shelter she'll push my hands away when I try – but this will be much later, and I shouldn't try. Her mother will say I'm no good, there's nothing much about me, too young and only after one thing. And I'll think of all the other times with Elsie and Bridget and Rosie Clifton. But I won't miss them, not really, not afterwards when she's gone home and I'm already licking the pencil and rummaging in my pockets for a scrap of paper to write her a letter and say *I'm sorry, forgive me, don't hate me May, please don't.*

Why doesn't anyone ever bring me anything to drink?

Someone praying. *Say Amen even if you don't understand.* Someone is calling my name. I should sober up. I should straighten up and fly right. Someone is saying my name but that place is where the knives are waiting and my eyes are sealed by light. The avenue of limes, the leaves all orange above and around me, my dad treading up and down inside a barrel of grapes. The dogs weaving in and around the trees. And Mum isn't dead like they told me, she's riding a bicycle in a purple dressing gown and carpet slippers. They can't see me. I'm invisible, just here absorbing the sun. I'll find her by the canal. She'll tell me what to do. She'll give me something to drink. My tongue will shrink back, suck in the water, turn pink. I'll be perfect. It's so clean. Was it always this clean? Jump in, and in the water the holes will close up, stitch themselves back. Everything mended. No more paper-cuts. Letterboxes everywhere. I hold up the shelf in Karen's room and feel the vibrations through my arm as she presses the power button on the drill. At the match I'll join the queue for a meat and potato pie. There's no rush. There's nothing, nothing but time.

Hands touching my hair. My eyes are still sealed. Mum with her hands in it, telling me, 'They're only jealous lad, they're jealous 'cause you light up every room.' And even if it wasn't true I decided to believe it, I decided to think it as I walked into every dancehall and cinema and office. And so it was. And when May finally said yes in the car by the river with the rain falling and the shadow of it reflected onto the dashboard, onto our hands and laps as though they were blank canvases just waiting for that moment of projection, I said 'I always knew you loved me. It was the hair wasn't it? No one could ever resist the hair.' She gave me the look then, called me a silly bugger and she was right. She was always right. And the gear-stick between us and my hand up her back underneath her bra strap and her nose on my nose and the exact familiar smell and taste of her.

This itching and the blanket too heavy on my chest, if I could shift myself I'd move over, put my weight on the other side because it feels as though all the flesh has melted and left just the bone, and the bone is aching, but I'm pinned down, there are no hands now, just the air and I'm stuck in it, my eyes are glued shut and the voices blur and merge and I can't get at anything I need, can't open my lips, this throat so dry – surely someone could do something. If she loved me she'd come and sort it all out. She'd find a way to stop the pain. But she doesn't. Never, never, never. It was all lies. Jim tried to warn me. He said I should be careful. He said *Take it from me Arthur, these women always turn into their mothers.* But not so soon. The cold-ness. Always pushing me away. I should've known and now this. Sitting against the bathroom door in the hotel room with her crying on the other side. Singing to her to try and get her to come out but she won't say anything. She won't tell me what's the matter. I try Sam Cooke: *At first I thought it was infatuation, but oooh it's lasted so long,* Pat Boone and the Banana

Boat Song. It always makes her laugh. My awful accent. *A beau-ti-ful bunch of ripe ban-na-nas!* I clench my fists. I want to break the door down. It's ridiculous – our wedding night and I'm sitting on the floor singing about tarantulas. This is what she's reduced me to. It's a terrible mistake, there's no universe inside her, just the promise of it. Stringing me along all this time, the frigid bitch, making me think there was more to it – looking down her nose and correcting my grammar. I think of Rosie Clifton, with her dark straight hair scraped up, giggling while she let me undo her buttons. Shake my head. The lock unclicks. Push myself up off the rough carpet, the pattern of it imprinted into my hand, one of my legs buzzing with pins and needles. I drag it across the lino and wait for the pain. *I'm bleeding* she says and looks me straight in the eye. Her face is raw with crying. There's no blood anywhere. Nothing makes sense. *I tried to work it all out but I'm not regular, I never have been, I get these pains* – I don't know what to say so I just hold her and this seems to work, this seems to be the right thing to do. And it's not the end of the world anymore. Just women's stuff. Things are postponed, not cancelled. I rub her back a bit and offer to buy her a nice big bag of chips.

But chips are no use now because my stomach isn't there, there's no place for them dripping fat and vinegar. If I retch I'll split apart and that'll be it, if I cough and swallow it'll never stop and the knives will come early, right now they're only pins hovering, ready to stick me if I move, but soon they'll get bigger and sharpen and –

May –

I think I've said it out loud but I can't be sure. My eyes, my eyelashes stuck together, I can open them a bit and when I do it's not the light like I expected but the dull grey of early evening – the curtains already closed, and the bowl next to the bed that I don't want to see and the smell of – and there's no one here. For a moment I think I can hear my mother downstairs humming the '1812 Overture' with Dad banging his fists on the table in place of all the cannons. That can't be right. If she'd only come I could make her laugh, I could make my voice work long enough to sing. I'd growl at her *Daylight come and we wan go home* and say *do me a favour – open the curtains will you love, and get me something to drink. Anything but water.* There are steps on the stairs now and it's her. Who else would it be? She'll be here and after the drink there'll be some kind of pill to take and I'll need to have a piss and to distract myself from it I'll say *Did you know they've stopped selling medicine in Boots?* And she'll say *The old ones are the best eh, Arthur?* And she'll help me sit up a little, just a little so that it prickles but doesn't cut, doesn't burn me in half like a laser in a James Bond film when they still had a bit of class about them. And I'll say *It's because the cough mixture was always leaking out through the lace holes.* It won't matter if she laughs or not. She'll sit with me as it goes dark and I'll feel her hands on me and as long as she's there I'll know that none of it – not one bit of it was imagined.

4:25 pm

Some parts of things are
lost. Some parts of things are hard to put your finger
on. But not the boy.

He's here.

He takes my hand.

Here is the church, here is the steeple. The boy
here, holding my hands.   Not a boy. Not a man.
His hair is like fire.   Here is the church, here is the steeple
doing something with my fingers. Maybe he can mend them
so many.

so clever!

I used to know things.

He has too many words. There didn't use to be this many
and Ned was never this big and he never came to church and
the church was not made out of hands but he has hair like fire
so he must be

the boy.

I used to splash in the puddles with Ned when I walked him
back to the farm. Love your neighbour, Dad said, but Mum
said everything has its limit. He has a family, she said. He has
a family of his own.

And this isn't him at all. I know that now. They want me to think so. Them. Always playing tricks. I don't want to play anymore. Give me back my hands.

This boy's not the right one at all.

29 March 2004

Alex

On the bus into town. The engine and the natterers in front drowning out the music. I should get some better headphones. We stop. The doors hiss and I wait for everyone to get out before sliding off the seat and saying cheers to the driver. Fresh air. The pavement speckled white. I can't tell whether it's meant to be like that or if it's just chewing gum spat out and trampled down.

He's there before I have time to change direction, right in front of me in his dirty sleeping bag. Back against the wall – paint peeling onto him like he's a permanent fixture. Matted hair, scruffy dog. All I have to do is walk past. I could cross over but the bus is pulling out. He won't speak to me. He won't. He doesn't. Doesn't even look up and I walk past feeling like shit anyway.

Ned would know exactly how to handle these situations. I imagine him like me but better. Like me but with posture and muscles and social skills. He carries extra fags and energy bars and his pockets jingle with spare change. He can hand these things over and not be a dick about it. That's why people want to be around him. That's why Nan's face changes when she realises I'm not him after all.

Town is heaving. If Mum hadn't taken the car I'd be at the supermarket or the retail park. Anywhere else. There are too many people. Push my way through Marks and Spencer's, past the fluffy dressing gowns and big knickers. Pick a card, any card. Pick something out of this line-up – something for less than a tenner. It's all generic mum stuff. As though spawning another human being means you're instantly drawn to knick-knacks and spotty tea towels, mugs with slogans so meaningless it makes me want to vom. Ned would know what to buy. He has excellent taste. He probably makes his own gifts.

Nan always used to sort this stuff out, buy me a card to sign, a present to wrap. Sometimes we went together. She'd peel five-pound notes from the wad she always had in her bank book and send me to the tills on my own. 'Go on,' she said, pushing me into the queue, 'you've got to learn to do these things on your own.' But it never gets easier. The small talk. The way the shop staff smile at you and pour change into your hand so the coins roll off and you have to bend over and balance the bag on your arm with everybody waiting behind.

There's enough money left for lunch. Meat and potato pasties are two for a pound. It doesn't make sense just to buy one. I grab a bottle of Coke and pay and find a bench near the war memorial even though it's still too cold to be sitting outside. Smells like fags and fried onions and a little bit of spring. The pastry grease is seeping through the paper bag. Two kids in front of me chasing pigeons – running and stamping and sending small flocks into the air to sit and wait in the trees, on the railings. A group of women in long black dresses, faces covered − only a slit cut out for eyes. A choir singing gospel through a shitty sound system and handing out leaflets about the *Good News*.

The Coke bubbles sting the back of my nose. I eat too quickly. It burns on the way down. Swig the drink again, watch a girl walk past, dyed hair piled up high on her head. She's wearing denim shorts with black tights underneath. From the back I can see everything, every crease and flex as she walks. She walks straight past the students with their little table and homemade posters, trying to collect signatures against the war in Iraq. She doesn't even look at them.

I feel for the postcard in my pocket and wonder what Lorna's doing at this very moment. I can't help myself. Pull it out and the corners are all dog-eared, the paper splitting and curling over. I know it off by heart. *Thomas Gainsborough, Cornard Wood.* Murky trees in oil paint. I can just see her in the shop at the National Gallery picking it out. Her writing on the back, tiny and perfect, taking up every inch of space so there is almost no room for the stamp. *The gathering of trees,* it says, *the poplars; the durmast oak; the soft lime-tree; the virgin sweet bay, laurel, the hazel, frail; the ash tree used for spears* and on and on. It could mean anything. There's no return address. Just like her to try and be mysterious. Quoting obscure lines from her set texts to feel clever. Sending me coded messages when she knows I was never good at reading between the lines. Today it feels like she's taking the piss. *The sweeping silver-fir; pleasant plane-tree; the many-coloured maple; with the river-haunting willow.* She laughed when I told her how scared I used to be of the yew trees in graveyards, how I imagined they were so dark because they soaked up evil spirits. And I always stepped around them when Nan took me to Church on Sunday mornings.

'Did you really believe it?' Lorna asked once, eager for details, like I was the last survivor of a dying tribe. And I just shrugged. I didn't know how to explain. Mostly it was boring. In Sunday school we made collages, filled shoeboxes for children in Romania, acted out scenes from the Bible. But sometimes – and I could never predict when – I felt this thing – this prickling in my face, my spine. Some kind of gut-twisting hope. Sort of like the Yorkshire caving trip in the last year before high school – fear of the dripping dark, sandwiched between people, hoping the fat kid in front wouldn't get stuck. Keeping the panic down by pretending you were a Power Ranger or Indiana Jones and breathing in the thick damp air. Not enough of it. Wondering what the hell it was all for, the sharp rock digging into your ribs, and then the first sniff of sky and light and the push forward.

Inasmuch as you have done it unto the least of these ye have done it verily, verily, verily, unto me. It has power, even when you hear it in that robot-vicar drone. A hot hand melting into you, into your body, moving things around, pushing. For a moment you want to jump up and do something. And then it goes and you forget. You're glad you didn't say anything embarrassing. You wonder whether you're turning into some kind of religious nut job.

Nan said faith is something that has to be fed and nurtured. 'It's a gift', she said, 'to hope for something more.' The Bible she gave me for my eighth birthday still has the plastic cover on. Sometimes when Mum's out I open it at random and try to find something familiar, something that might bring the feeling back.

I can't think about any of it now. Not Lorna, or the others. Everyone I ever went to school with leaving town and spreading out across the country like arrows on a map. Invasion. Escape. I'm still hungry. I could eat the other pasty easily, but I don't. I get up and start walking back towards the bus stop, past what used to be Pizza Hut and now doubles as a shitty Christmas shop and a temporary place to buy fireworks. Past the sports shop with trashy dance playlist – all drum machines and over-produced vocals. You have to wear branded tracksuit bottoms to be allowed in. It's a legal requirement. Past the man who always sits on a stool outside BHS playing French love songs on the accordion.

I'm holding the bag so the grease doesn't get all over the other stuff. The pasty's going cold. I want rid of it. All I have to do is hand it over. Say *Here you go mate*, as though I do things like this every day – as if it means nothing. And not wait around to see his reaction, not look as though I'm waiting for gratitude. My palms are sweating. I feel shivery and wired, like I'm about to sit an exam. Maybe he's not hungry. Maybe I should've bought him a drink as well. Nothing worse than being thirsty and the food sticking in your throat. Maybe he's a fucking vegetarian.

I stop and breathe and look like I'm really interested in the nearest shop window, the cheap pyjamas and cushions shaped like cupcakes and chocolates wrapped in shiny pink cellophane. Don't forget your Mum on Mother's Day, and the date in big bold letters to really hammer it home. Time is running out, people, buy now, buy here!

We made a hamper together one Christmas. Nan knew the wife of a man who'd lost his job. They had nothing. So we went to town and chose fruit and nuts and biscuits and a box of Milk Tray and some children's gloves from the market, some colouring pencils and big fat cheapo colouring books. And we wrapped the toys and arranged it all in a big cardboard box covered with Christmas paper. I bit off small strips of Sellotape and handed them over. It was heavy. They lived round the corner and I walked next to her while she carried it, stopping to steady herself against the houses. I could've sworn that all the curtains on the street were twitching. When we were near she handed it to me and I thought I might drop it for laughing. We peered round the side wall and saw a light on in the back of the house. 'Go – now,' she said and I shuffled as fast as I could and put it on the doorstep and the glass bottle of cordial clanked against the metal tin of Fox's Family Assortment and I rang the doorbell and ran and she held my hand and we legged it back to her house.

A couple of weeks later, after church, a man I'd never seen before pushed his way through the crowd and spoke to Nan. He'd been trying to find out who did it, he said, and he knew it was her and while he was very grateful indeed for the thought there was no way he could accept it. And he pushed a ten-pound note into her hand and walked off. She just stood there for a while, we both did, and her cheeks were red, and then we went back for Sunday dinner, waiting for Mum to pick me up on her way home from work.

It fizzled out after that. She stopped taking me and I never said anything. I missed it but I didn't miss it. We played board games while the roast was cooking, watched *Songs of Praise* after and sang along. I peed myself laughing at the congregations – their eager faces, so filled with spiritual fire that they couldn't contain it.

The bus'll be coming soon and there's not another for half an hour. It's now or never. I need to stop messing about and just do it. Put my headphones back in and walk, walk, walk to the beat of the song and feel like I can do anything. And I look up to the top of the buildings, some concrete and ugly and others towering over the shops with art deco cornices and long Georgian windows. Gargoyles on the old Bradford & Bingley. A whole hidden world above the sale signs and new season beachwear and stylised headless mannequins.

Cross the road, weaving through turning traffic and plastic carrier bags hanging off prams and I can see him sitting in the same place by the wall and I can hear a train pulling into the station and the sun is out now, breaking through the grey.

He's not alone. There's someone next to him bending over the dog, scratching its ears, a man in biker leathers with a grey ponytail and massive sideburns. They're laughing at something and he nods and the man in leathers salutes him like he's a washed up ship's captain who just happened to land on a pavement outside a train station.

I could still do it. I could just drop it onto his sleeping bag and keep walking. And I'm right there and it's now or never. Now, now, now.

Fuck it. I walk straight past him.

I'm not hungry anymore. I can't eat it. So I leave the paper bag on the chopping board next to the toaster. I take Lorna's postcard out of my pocket and screw it up in both hands. I hover next to the bin but can't actually bring myself to do it. There might be something I haven't spotted yet. A hidden message or even an apology. I take it upstairs and unfold it. The trees are criss-crossed with papery lines now. Some of the words are almost unreadable.

I slot it into the Bible and shove it under the bed. Turn on the computer and wait for it to boot up. Try not to look at the wreckage, the state of my bombs-dropped-pig-sty-hovel. Staring at the screen with the cursor blinking in the Google search box. The whole world at my fingertips and I can't think of a single thing to type.

I hear the car pull into the drive and the door go. I count to twenty slowly. I hear Mum dropping bags in the hall, hanging up the keys, filling the kettle. Her feet on the stairs. By nineteen she's knocking on the door and opening it just a bit, peering in like she's testing the atmosphere, measuring hostility levels.

'Alright?' she says – she has this tone. I'm delicate. I might explode.

'Fine.'

'There's a pasty in the kitchen.'

'They were on offer ok – cheap as chips so I brought one back.'

'For me?'

'Who else?'

She's still there. Why is she hovering around? She smiles. More than that – she bloody lights up.

'How did you know? I'm starving. Just what I fancied.'

'Don't overdo it. It's just a pie.' She should save her enthusiasm. There's some serious pastel Mother's Day shit heading her way in only a matter of hours. She looks at me looking at the screen.

'What're you doing?' she says, moving closer like she might actually sit on the bed, like she wants to *connect*.

'Working on an application.'

'What for?'

'Just a job. At a restaurant. Something to tide me over.'

She wants to mention university now. I can feel it.

'That's something at least.' She hovers. 'Have you heard from Lorna lately?'

'Mum!'

'I'm just asking.'

'Well, don't.'

'I was thinking of getting a takeaway later and watching a film. What d'you think?'

'Dunno. I'm pretty busy here.'

She retreats to the door. She's almost gone.

'If you change your mind…' she says.

I nod, but it's not going to happen and she knows it.

The door shuts. She's gone and I can breathe, but I can't breathe. I don't know why it's like this. I don't know why I'm like this. I don't know what I want. I don't want anything.

Nan in the home, turning away or staring at my forehead when I try to talk to her, as if there's always something more interesting going on behind me. As if she's waiting for someone better. Waiting for Ned. And that girl comes in and she wakes up, she focuses. Not on me, on her. The girl with the dark hair. Her name is something exotic. Anita. Brigitte. *Sinita*. What does it matter? There's no one. There's nothing.

Push the chair back and climb into bed, right under the duvet so that I can't see any light, so that I'm breathing in my own air, nails into the palms of my hands, elbows into my stomach. It starts in my head. The words: *Verily I say unto you, even as I am. Come follow me. Come. Follow.*

Then I whisper it: *Please God, please God, please God*, and outside a bird is singing and the light must be going and the air is getting hotter under here and please God I don't know how I'll ever move from this spot.

5:03 pm

Something is altogether wrong. There are doors that never open. Things I can't get hold of.

Here is the church, here is the steeple.   Oh come ye, oh come ye to Be-eth-lehem.   Here is the church, here is the   church.

          That church.   The seats were hard. Like rock. Kneeling down, getting up. My bum went numb. Mum pinched my leg because I couldn't keep my bottom still. The coffin was so very tiny. Dad had his head down for the whole thing. Right down on his knees. He wouldn't look. I poked him on the shoulder because I wanted him to sit up straight and help me find the hymn. He wouldn't move. Not until everyone else was gone.

          There was a boy – there was definitely a boy.

          I'm starting to think he's not coming.

6 May 2006

Afsana

A million and one things to do, but first I have to show them the room. I lead them past the reception desk and down the corridor. Keep turning round to smile, to slow down and make sure they're following.

'Did you hear that George?' the woman – Margaret – says, 'we're going to look at your new bedroom.'

George has his stick in one hand, but he's leaning on his wife, his left arm through hers, moving forward and looking at his feet – *left, right, left, right* – as though every bit of energy he's got has to be focused on keeping himself upright. Nothing to spare for talking. I'm waiting for them to catch up. Trying not to stare. One side of his face is slack. His eyelid droops. He has two days' stubble, and his trousers are bunched up, pulled tight at the waist, hanging loose everywhere else. He needs feeding and washing and sorting out. God knows how she's managed this long.

I unlock the door and step into the room. All the light from the window spills out onto the corridor in a line, like a golden footpath leading them in. I can smell disinfectant from the en-suite. The cover on the bed folded over in tight little corners. The standard bedside cabinet and the emergency button.

Nothing personal. Nothing that means anything. We'll bring his bags in later, while he's in the lounge. By the time we put him to bed it'll feel like home. That's the theory anyway.

Margaret tries to guide him through the doorway but he holds back. He's unsteady. I wait by the bed wondering if I should intervene. He leans on his stick and pulls away from her.

'Here we are,' she says, 'it's not so bad. Nice and clean and a bit of green through the window to cheer you up. There's space for all your things and I'll come everyday and –' he pulls away and grunts. It might be a word. It might be a 'no'. 'Please love, just come in. For me. Please.'

He won't budge. He drops the walking stick and grabs onto the doorframe. That noise again.

'George,' she says, and she's pulling him now, hard enough that if she lets go I'm afraid she'll topple over backwards. Her tiny wrists and ankles. I should do something but it feels too private. I want to turn away so she won't know I've witnessed it all. This is my job. I have to make it better.

'It's ok,' I say and move forward and hold both his arms at the top, almost under his armpits. All bones and sinew. He doesn't look at me. He doesn't resist. Margaret lets go and I take his weight. My forehead's almost resting on the top of his head. He smells of aftershave. Strong and sharp. His hair – what's left of it – needs a good brush. I have to be patient. Rushing him won't work. It's like in films sometimes when a scruffy kid manages to tame a wild horse just by holding its head and standing close and being calm. If you feel it they'll feel it too. His body relaxes. Margaret hands me the stick and I give it back to him. He takes it. We move forward towards the bed. His arm through my arm like he's walking me down the aisle. It's not too far. I look down at the carpet to try and see what he's seeing. Little purple flecks and diamonds that carry on forever. If you stare long enough it looks like they're moving. I turn him around. 180 degrees. I ask him, quietly, to bend his knees. I have to repeat it a few times and push at his thighs a little before he gives and then he lets himself fall from too high and the bed bounces when his bum hits it and he breathes out in shock, and the sound vibrates. He looks at me. Straight at me. His eyes are blue and bloodshot and watery. It's like he wants to tell me something. There's something he needs me to know. I stand up and let Margaret take my place.

'Thank you,' she says.

I can't hold her gaze for long. She sits down and takes his hand and strokes it. She moves closer so their shoulders are touching. He doesn't look at her and she doesn't seem to expect anything more. Her skirt has ridden up to her knees exposing the top of her pop-socks. Too orange. The material's cutting into her calf. A line of mottled blue skin exposed to the air.

'Stay here for as long as you need,' I say, 'just press the buzzer and someone will come to fetch you for tea and biscuits.'

Walking down the corridor and into the lounge it's like leaving a sacred space. Putting your shoes back on and stepping out of a mosque and back into the real world. A wall of demands. The noise. The music. Everybody wants something. I think about Dadi. I wonder whether Amina's still at home ladling out her endless cups of chai. Doubtful. She wanted to go to university. She wanted to go to Birmingham and study Law. Now I think about it, it was never Baba who showed us the photographs and letters from Pakistan. It was Mum. She didn't understand Urdu so she must've got Baba to read them to her late at night after work. She showed us the pages and told us second-hand news about the farm and the never-ending supply of cousins. Always getting married. Dropping like flies. She wanted us to know about them. She wanted us to feel part of a bigger family. There was a photograph she'd framed before we were born. It was her favourite. Baba on the day before he flew to England. I can still see it. He's standing in a field wearing a white kurta. His face is smooth and he's shading his eyes from the sun. Dadi stands next to him with her head down, her hair parted in exactly the same place although most of it's hidden underneath a patterned dupatta. The image is black and white but you can tell it's hot. The sky is different. The light.

'She want him here,' Mum said touching Baba's face with her index finger, 'to keep him safe from all the fighting.'

'Ow! Watch it, Sana.'

I collide with Alison as she comes round the corner.

'Sorry. I was somewhere else.'

She stops and rubs her shoulder.

'Away with the fairies as usual. How's the new arrival?'

She doesn't wait for an answer. She's holding a pile of paperwork. Always in the middle of something. Never still for more than a few seconds.

'This is for you.'

She hands me a fat brown envelope.

'What is it?'

'An NVQ information pack.'

'Alison... I told you. I'm not –'

'Just do it, Sana. You're a natural, I'm telling you. A bit of paperwork, a couple of essays, and the world's your lobster. Well, not exactly the *world*, but you know what I mean. It's a start. It's more money. What's to think about?'

'I don't know.'

'Just take it ok? Fill in the application. You can thank me later.'

I take it. The flap of the envelope is ripped where it's been opened. There are bits of fluff all along the sticky strip. She smiles at me. She has no idea. I feel sick suddenly. I can't focus. Everything's blurred. Rushing towards me.

'Are you alright?'

I put a hand out to steady myself.

'Sana?'

I shake my head to clear it. Concentrate. Re-focus.

'I need some fresh air. Just for a few minutes.'

She looks around, back towards the office to check if Gill's within earshot. Nothing. All the staff are busy elsewhere.

'Go,' she says, 'I'll cover for you.'

I stuff the envelope into my locker, slip my coat on and push the staff door outwards. Air. Breathe it in. It's raining but I don't feel it at first. There's a delay, like somebody's sheltering me from the wet. A giant hand. My own invisible umbrella. Then it breaks through. Water hitting my face, finding its way under my hood. Like when Amina used to flick her toothbrush at me before bed and dare me to tell. I run over to the smoking shelter. The sky is dark, like the light just gave up and let evening come early. Stand as far in as I can, my back against the rough bricks. Knuckles catching on the edge of them. I look at my hands. Not bleeding, just scraped white. I close my eyes and swallow the nausea down and try to calculate whether there could be a baby. Unlikely, but not impossible. Oh God, please let it be impossible. There's someone coming over. A man. I can't make out a face. The rain is too heavy. He's tall. His coat is draped over his head. If I go now it'll look rude. I don't want to make small talk. I want to be alone. He sees me and stops. He stands outside the shelter getting wet. I move along to make it clear there's room. He steps in.

'Sorry,' he says.

I don't know what he's sorry for. He hasn't done anything. He puts his coat on properly. It's too big on him. That hair though. Golden. Red. Somewhere in between. The only bright thing in a sea of grey. I'm staring. Look away. Say something.

'You can smoke if you want to. I'm going in in a minute.'

He shakes his head. 'No, it's fine. I don't want to, I mean – I don't even – it's fine, really.'

'You're May's grandson, right?'

'Yeah.'

'She talks about you.'

'Really?'

'The boy with the red hair.'

'She calls me Ned.'

'What's your name?'

'Alex.'

'Ah. Who's Ned?'

'I have no idea.'

He stares out at the car park, like he's longing to get away. There are things I could tell him about her. Last week she followed me into the corridor, holding her bag against her body like her life depended on it. She stopped me and whispered in my ear.

'Can you make use of this?' she said.

She opened the bag and separated a tissue off the pile stuffed into the front pocket. She looked around as if she was afraid we were being watched.

'Don't tell anyone or they'll all want some.'

I took it. It was easier. She kept pulling them out. Some of the sheets separating until they were almost see-through. One after another, after another. 'Treat yourself to something nice,' she said.

'Weather turned out nice again,' Alex says.

For a minute it doesn't register. I'm about to nod and then I see his face and we both laugh. He looks even younger when he smiles. The staff door blows open and there's a quick blast of Glenn Miller, 'String of Pearls.' It's too upbeat and I've heard it too often. They must be serving tea already and I really should be helping inside. The sky goes even darker, like someone's twisting a dimmer switch, and then the hail starts, great stinging globs of it coming in diagonally, hitting us in the face. For God's sake. I'm laughing now and so's he and I reach out without thinking and hold onto his arm to steady myself and we both go to pull our hoods up at the exact same moment and turn towards the wall. I can't breathe. Like when Baba used to tickle me under the chin before bed and his fingers were too rough and it went on for too long. I wanted him to stop, but not to go away. Everything's a bit too close, too intimate. Both of us laughing like idiots. His fingers so long and thin. The nails bitten down to the quick.

'Bloody hell,' he says. 'Is someone trying to tell us something?'

They are, I want to say, except he'd think I'm crazy. Everything feels like a sign. The new couple and the envelope and the weather and this moment right now. Someone's trying to tell me something, even if I don't want to hear it. Whatever's meant to be will be, Insha'Allah. Do the best with what you're given. Keep moving forward on the right path. God willing. Allah permitting. I start to laugh again. I can't keep it back. It's taking over. The hails stops as quickly as it started and leaves us with the rain again. We stand apart. It's not funny anymore. He's just standing there looking at me. My eyes are streaming and I try to wipe them and thank God I've never been bothered with makeup. There are tears mixed up with it and I don't know whether I'm crying or laughing.

'Are you ok?'

I nod, then shake my head. I don't know how to answer that, but I have to say something. I have to try.

'The thing is, Alex —' I stop and swallow because my voice is all squeaky and embarrassing, 'the thing is — don't think I'm a nutcase or anything — oh God, I'm sorry —'

I can't stop and between the tears I look at him and he seems like he's in actual pain. His cheeks going red. He moves forward then back on his heels. He must think I'm off my trolley. But he doesn't leave and there's something about him that makes me want to just blurt everything out.

'I'm ok, honestly. I mean, my life's a mess, but I'm not crazy or anything. I promise.' Take a big shaky breath.

'What happened?'

'It's hard to explain.'

'You don't have to —'

'No. I want to. It's just complicated. Here's the thing Alex — do you have a girlfriend?'

His cheeks go pink again. He shakes his head.

'I've been with my boyfriend for the best part of ten years. Unbelievable. And he wants to get married. He's wanted to for a while actually. He wants to have kids.'

'Right.'

'And I keep putting it off — waiting for the right time. But today there was this new couple who came in, and the man was in a bad way. He should've been here ages ago. And the way she held onto him, you know? The way she looked at him. Still. And I thought *that's* what it should be like. And if it isn't – if it can't be, then what am I even doing? Does that make any sense?'

'Yes.'

'But it's so complicated.'

'Yep.'

'And something's got to change.'

He nods.

I look at him again. His pale eyelashes. He's probably uncomfortable. Came out to get some fresh air, to be alone, to *think*, and look what he got instead. I'm calm now. I'm back in control.

'What about you?' I say.

'My mum thinks I'm gay.'

It's so unexpected I can't do anything but laugh. Thank God he's laughing too.

'I'm sorry. That's not funny.'

'It sort of is though. She's obsessed.' He runs his hand through his hair and tries to look serious. 'Not that there's anything wrong with being gay.'

'Of course not,' I say it as if it's obvious. As if I hadn't lived half my life thinking the exact opposite.

'But I'm not.'

'Right.'

'So.'

'Excellent.'

We're laughing again and I fish out a half-used tissue from my pocket and blow my nose. The rain has calmed down now.

A soft patter on the plastic roof. I can hear the music from inside. A murmur of voices.

'A blackbird,' he says.

'What?'

'Over there. Listen.'

He points to a big tree in the corner of the car park, hanging over the fence from someone's garden. I can't see the bird, but the sound it makes suddenly cuts through the rain and the wet rush of cars on the road. High and sharp. Clear notes fading into a trill. It was background before but now it's impossible to hear anything else. We stand silently for a few seconds. The pattern of it. The pause and then the same song, over and over.

'They like singing after rain,' he says.

'It's still raining.'

'Maybe they know it's going to stop.'

I look at him and he meets my eye for the first time, prop-erly, without looking nervous, without pretending to be interested in the peeling stickers on the shelter, the cigarette butts on the floor. He smiles.

'I should be getting back,' I say, 'they'll be sending out a search party.'

He nods. He pushes the gravel around with his shoe. My stomach's aching from laughing so much. The nausea's still there but it's not as bad. The blackbird still singing. I want to say something about May but it's not my place. I want to say *She's different every day. Don't take it personally. Just talk to her. Keep trying. Ask her about Ned.*

'See you inside,' he says.

Back in the lounge they've moved onto Frank Sinatra. May's asleep in her chair by the radiator. I step right into the action as though I've never been away. *Let me see what spring is like on Jupiter and Mars.* Alison winks at me from the corner. They sing. It's always surprising. People you can't get any sense out of suddenly open up and sing all the words as though they haven't got a problem with forgetting after all. I look around for George and Margaret. He's in a chair over by the door shaking his head and pushing her arm away. He isn't singing. He's saying something but I can't hear it above the music. It might not even be words. I walk over and crouch down in front of him so he can see my face. I put my hand on his leg to let him know I'm here but it's the wrong thing to do. He kicks his leg out hard and catches me right on my thigh. It's a reflex. It's not personal but it feels personal. The pain. I feel sick again for a minute and have to stand up and bend over.

'George!' she's saying it over and over, but he won't look at her and Alison is next to me before I know it.

'Ok,' she says, 'Are you hurt, Sana?'

I rub my leg and wave her away. It's not a big deal.

'What's his name again?' she leans in so Margaret won't hear her.

'George.'

'Ok, George. Shall we take a walk? Shall we go somewhere a bit quieter?'

He rocks back and forward and makes a wailing sound that could mean anything. She takes it as a yes. I help her to lift him out the chair. We're both on edge in case he hits out again, but there's no resistance. We walk him through the door and it swings shut behind us and in the corridor there's only the ghost of the song and the rain hitting the fire door and he breathes out as if he's relieved. Margaret's wiping tears out of her eyes with a proper cotton hanky.

'Don't worry,' I say, 'it takes time to settle in. It's new, that's all.'

'I don't want to leave him.'

'You can come as often as you want,' Alison says, so matter-of-fact, so sure of the right thing. 'Go home now and sleep. Get some rest and things will look better in the morning.'

It's meaningless really. But it's what she needs to hear.

We settle him in his room and shut the door behind us. We just stand there and look at each other for a minute.

'Another satisfied customer.'

'Don't make me laugh. Seriously. I'm on the edge today as it is.'

'We've got medication for that, Sana.'

'Stop it.'

'How's your leg?'

'I'll live.'

'Do we need to fill out an incident form?'

'It's hardly life-threatening.'

'Procedures must be followed.'

'I'm not going to sue, I promise.'

'You wouldn't have a leg to stand on.' She looks at me, waggles her eyebrows up and down.

I laugh. 'That's terrible.'

'Whatever gets me through the day.'

We stop by the staff room. My shift's almost over. I'll get wet waiting for the bus. I'll have to listen to Ewan summarising his OFSTED preparations over dinner. Staffroom politics and paranoia. My stomach rumbles and I put my hand on it, suck it in to try and control the noise. I won't have anything to say that he'll want to hear. A dull ache in my groin, in the pit of my stomach, like there always is this time of the month. A good sign. Please God, a good sign.

Five minutes to go. There's no point going back in the lounge, I'll only get kept past my time. The phone rings and Alison disappears into the office to answer it. I lean against the wall and press on my thigh. It's sore. There'll be a big bruise tomorrow. I think about the way Dadi held my arm that day at the train station. It was only supposed to be Amina bringing me some things. I'd sworn her not to tell them where I was. I wasn't going back to Leicester, that's all they needed to know. I wasn't going to be buried alive at home and then shipped off to Pakistan to marry some relative who looked like he was still living in the 1970s. I should've run when I saw her face pressed up against the glass. Amina was nowhere to be seen. Dadi waited for a minute after the doors opened. She just stood there in the train doorway, right on the edge holding everyone up. She was wearing her best outfit. Maroon silk. It was cool that day but she didn't have a coat. Maybe she was waiting for me to help her. Maybe she'd never needed to get off a train on her own before. All the other passengers started pushing forward. She tutted at them and stepped down and walked over to me. She stood too close. I couldn't look at her. She grabbed my arm and her fingers dug in.

'We wait here for the next train,' she said, 'and then we go.'

I wanted to tell her the next train from that particular platform would just take us further in the wrong direction. I shook my head instead.

'No?'

'No.'

'Enough, Afsana. Come now and he won't have to find out. Stay here and there's no going back, you understand? You'll break his heart. Is that what you want?'

'No.'

'Come then.'

'I can't.'

'What's this can't? You can. You will. Show me the way.'

She started walking towards the exit, dragging me with her. She stopped in front of the flashing timetables, squinting up.

'Which platform?'

'Platform two, but I'm not coming.'

'You are.'

'I can't. I'm sorry.'

She stood in front of me then and held both my arms and shook me like I was still a child. 'What are these tears for? Do you understand Afsana? Do you understand what you're doing?'

'Yes, and I'm sorry, but I still can't come.'

She wiped her eyes. I'd never seen her cry before. I felt like I was going to be sick. People were staring at us. The mangled sound of the train announcer. *The twelve forty-five to London Euston is now approaching platform three.*

'I'll ring the police,' she said, 'I'll ring them this minute.'

'It won't do any good.'

She stood away from me and turned around so I couldn't see her face, wiping her hand over her headscarf. When she turned back she was calmer.

'I'm going to the platform now,' she said. 'I want you to stay here and think. Think of your home and your Baba and how your own mother would've felt if she could see you. Probably she's watching you now from heaven, and willing you to make the right choice. Think of what you're doing to Amina. Think of your selfishness. Think where these actions are leading you. I'll wait there until the next train and if you don't join me, if you don't make the sensible choice and come home then Allah Yusa'amah. I can do no more.'

She didn't ask me for an address or a phone number. She didn't ask me about *him*. It was all or nothing. Now or never. I watched her climb the steps to the platform. I watched until she was out of sight and then I ran straight for the exit.

I hear Alison hanging up the phone. I put my head round the office door.

'I'm heading off now.'

'You sure you're ok? Are you feeling any better?'

'I'm fine. It's just – Alison? Could I stay with you, if I ever needed to – if there was an emergency I mean?'

I don't know where it comes from. I wasn't planning to say it. She's taken aback. I never ask her for anything. I never take up any of her offers.

'Sana – what's happened? What's he done to you?'

'No – it's nothing. Honestly. It's nothing like that. I just think I might need to get away. I mean, it might be nothing, it might just be hormones, but I think… I can't explain it –'

She puts a hand on my arm. 'Say the word and I'll send my Dave over with the van.'

The kindness. So straightforward. She means it. I laugh. I might cry again. I want to hug her but I don't. I want to say thank you but I can't speak. It's ok though. It doesn't matter. She understands.

6:55 pm

If I tell the girl then the message will be safe. She's the only one.

I pretended to be asleep. I sat on the stairs and looked through the
bars He was kneeling at her feet. He was kneeling like in a story. But they were already married. So it was something else he was asking for. He was pulling on her skirt. He was saying *please, please, please.* First the boy was lost and then Dad.

She wouldn't look at him. I wanted her to look at him. I wanted her to make him stay.

She always told him off for whistling in the house. She never even liked the way he sang.

19 October 1977

Karen

Dad's music seeping in from the hallway – all that twangy cowboy crap and Mum singing along under her breath even though she claims she doesn't like it either. She's whisking the Yorkshire pudding mix in the big plastic jug. The smell of the beef cooking in the oven makes my stomach hurt. All my school books spread out across the kitchen table. She'll be asking me to put them away anytime now so she can put the cutlery out for lunch.

I can't concentrate. I'm too hungry. Stare down at the blank page and suck the end of my pencil. Lead poisoning might buy me a day off school and it'd be worth it just to get out of woodwork. My mind is a blank. I can't remember what Mr Reynolds said about the design brief. The sketches are due in for tomorrow and I've got nothing. I write my name over and over. Karen Whittaker. K Whittaker. K W. If I married Simon Williams I wouldn't have to change my initials. Claire would roll her eyes. She wouldn't be seen dead with a boy from our year. Not even Simon. 'He's well fit,' she said once, 'but he knows it. And you should never trust a boy with longer eyelashes than you.'

If I hadn't listened to Claire I wouldn't be in this mess. But we were too busy laughing at Mr Reynolds. The way he talks, how he can't pronounce his R's at all. And Claire with that look on her face. The kind that means she's going to get me into trouble. She got up and sneaked to the back of the classroom while he was writing on the board. Someone cleared their throat but he was clueless. She landed back in her seat just as he turned round. Chalk-dust on his chin. He looked down at the textbook, turned back and started writing again. Claire passed me something under the desk. A smooth wooden handle.

'Careful, it's heavy,' she said.

I looked down. Some kind of wood file. Long and thin, the metal plate like a mega cheese grater. I rested it on my knee and she passed me another one.

'Rasps,' she said, 'I dare you.'

Reynolds was saying something about design and precision, about selecting the right tools for the job. Claire whispered instructions in my ear. I hesitated. She nudged me. So I did it. I held them up – one in each hand – and tapped them against each other. They hardly made a sound. She rolled her eyes. *Go on.* So I pulled. One against the other, as hard as I could. Metal scraping against metal. The screech and the shudder of it. It set my teeth on edge. I could feel the vibrations in my gums. Around the class people were groaning and covering their ears. Mr Reynolds span around and his eyes were wild, his face all pink. Claire looked like all her Christmases had come at once.

'Kawen Whittaker!' he yelled, 'put those down wight now,'

he took a big gulping breath, 'you never, ever wub the wasps together!'

Claire laughed so hard she snorted.

'Sorry, sir,' I said, trying to look calm. I put them down on the desk.

From the back of the class someone repeated his line in a squeaky voice. All the W's instead of R's. He stood there for a minute, not saying anything and the bell rang for break. Chairs scraping on the tiles, bag zips and all the laughing. Someone said 'Thank you Mr Weynolds' in a singsong voice and Claire grabbed my hand to pull me away. We pushed out into the corridor and legged it as fast as we could, ignoring him calling me to stay behind.

'He's a stupid, soft get,' Claire said when we made it out onto the yard, 'don't worry, he won't do nothing.'

Someone hit me on my shoulder. I turned round to push them back but it was Simon Williams grinning at me, his white shirt unbuttoned at the neck and hanging out of his trousers on one side. He gave me the thumbs up.

'Nice one, Karen,' he said, 'classic.'

There wasn't time to say anything back. I just smiled like an idiot and he was gone. Claire elbowed me in the ribs.

'Nice one, Karen,' she said and my face went hot. She put on a low, husky voice. 'Classic.'

'Get lost.'

'Ka-wen Whittaker, are you blushing?'

This bloody music. Better than the hymns at church, but not

by much. I wish I had earplugs. The door bangs open and Dad skids into the kitchen. He shuts it behind him and leans back to keep it closed.

'Bloody hell, May, there's a bird walking around in the dining room.'

I sit up. The look on his face. He's properly scared. Mum is draining vegetables in a colander over the sink. 'Why don't you open a window?' she says without turning round.

'You should see the size of it. It's almost as big as Karen.'

'I didn't know ostriches were native to Lancashire.'

'Stop joking, woman and come and do something about it!'

She turns around and her cheeks are all flushed, her hair frizzy from the steam. 'Can you not see I'm busy here. Cooking a roast dinner's a delicate balance and it's not like I get any help.'

'Come on!' he says, 'I'm telling you. It was staring at me with its beady little eyes.'

'For goodness' sake!'

I cover my mouth so he won't catch me laughing. Push the chair back across the lino. Mum wipes her hands on a tea towel.

'You can stay here and clear that mess off the table,' she says with her hand on the back of my chair, then pushes past and opens the door.

I ignore her and follow them both into the hall. Dad grips my wrist with his big rough fingers and I'm about to tell him to get off but the bird is there. Black and white and bigger than I expected. Not an ostrich, but solid enough and totally out of place. It's walking in circles on the carpet in the hallway, just stalking around, taking everything in.

'I told you,' he said.

'It's just a magpie.'

'Well get it out.'

There's a flash of metallic blue as it turns towards us. I laugh. Finally, something interesting happening in this bloody house. Dad lets go of my arm and stands behind me.

'Must've come down the chimney,' Mum says.

'I don't care where it came from. Get it out before it shits on the sofa!'

'Arthur! Go and open the back door if you want to help.'

I can't stop now, I'm laughing so hard no sound is coming out. My stomach hurts with it. My eyes are starting to water. I take a breath and manage to speak.

'Good morning, Mr Magpie,' I say and salute the bird.

Mum's walking strangely, hunched and slow like a cowboy, like she's squaring up, getting ready to take it on. 'It's the middle of the afternoon,' she says, 'and stop hovering behind me, you're not helping.'

'It's coming for you, Dad,' I shout, and Mum herds the bird past my legs through the doorway into the kitchen. It flaps up on top of the cereal cupboard and the sound of its wings, the size of it's too much. A breeze from the back door cutting through the heat from the oven. Dad's holding a chair out in front of him in self-defence. The bird settles there for a moment, unconcerned, just having a good nosy around.

'Look at its eyes,' he says, 'just look.'

'What exactly do you think it's going to do to you?'

'I don't know. Nothing good. Where are your rings, May? It'll be looking for treasure.'

And then it leaves. Just like that. Flaps down and saunters out the back door.

And everything is back to normal. The dregs of lunch. Dad tips his plate up and scrapes the last of the gravy off with a spoon. He's already yawning. I can feel it setting in early. The Sunday night dreads. Soon he'll be lying on the sofa for a nap and it'll be the sound of the clock ticking in the hallway. Worse than Willy Nelson, worse than the old women at church who know the words to all the hymns and warble their way through the choruses, sliding right up to the high notes. Blank pages to fill. Clean uniform laid out on my bed. Everything in its rightful place.

Mum gets up and opens the oven to check the crumble. There's a noise from the hall, a pause while I listen out and then it comes again. A knock on the door.

'Who the bloody hell is that?'

'Language, Arthur.'

'I'll get it.'

I leave them at the table and run through the hall. Three giant leaps. Open the door and it's Claire standing there with her new jeans on and her hands in her pockets.

'Glory, glory, Hallelujah.'

'That bad is it?' she says.

'What do you think?'

'Coming out then?'

'Too right. Just give me a minute.'

I grab my coat and slip my shoes on. Look at the clock. We can go to the park and still have time to catch the Top Twenty at Claire's after. I run back to the kitchen but before I can say anything Mum gives me the look.

'Where do you think you're going?'

'Claire's.'

'No you're not,' she says, 'not unless you've finished that homework.'

'I finished it. I did it before tea.'

'You didn't. The page is still blank. I checked.'

I kick at the table leg. Even with my shoes on it jars my toe. I want to tell her to her face she's a stupid cow but I swallow it down. 'She's going to help me with the homework. We'll do it together.'

'I said no, Karen. Tell her you'll see her tomorrow then come and sit down for some pudding.'

There's no give in her voice. I look at Dad but he just shrugs. He's holding his spoon and waiting for her to dish him up some crumble. I want to scream. I walk back to the door. Claire rolls her eyes. No need to explain, she heard every word.

'See you tomorrow, then,' she says and walks off down the road. I watch her till she's out of sight. The pockets on her bum in the shape of love hearts. Her bag banging on her hip.

Back in the kitchen they're acting like nothing's the matter. Mum puts a bowl in front of me but I push it away. They talk about nothing. Stupid stuff. The woman on the next street who fell and broke her hip. The fact that the milkman missed the extra pint off the order on Friday.

'I don't know if we'll have enough for breakfast now,' Mum says.

You should call the Evening Post, I think, *they might change Monday's headlines.*

'Are you not eating that?' Dad says.

I shove the bowl over to his side of the table. I look at Mum. 'I could've done my homework this morning if you hadn't made me go to church.'

'You could've done it on Saturday if you hadn't been so busy watching rubbish on the television.'

I want to throw a pea down the front of her Sunday blouse or pull the tablecloth out from under all the plates like they do on the TV. She's still talking but I'm not taking it in. All the plates and bowls smashing into pieces on the floor, the jug of custard tipped over into her lap.

'You can't blame everything on other people,' she says, 'sometimes you have to take responsibility for your own mistakes.'

★

I put the radio on but I can still hear them through the floor. The sound of the plates as she washes up, the cupboard doors shutting as he puts them away. I jump up and down a few times and the floor vibrates. They go quiet but no one comes up the stairs. And then their voices again. My homework's still a blank page. This is a day of rest. Kick the book across the room and lie face down on the bed. Bury my head in the pillow, hold my breath and start to count. Like the woman who got battered to death on Corrie last year. The actress lying there pretending to be dead. Trying to look stiff and make her breathing invisible. Hold on until all the air is gone, until there's nothing else but the need for it. They don't understand that everything about this place is yesterday's news.

I try to imagine what it must be like to have money. Like Claire's sister, working on the cheese counter at Booths to save up for a trip round Europe.

'That's what it's about,' she said one night, coming into Claire's bedroom in her long green skirt. She smelt of incense sticks. Her toenails were painted blue. 'It isn't about the money. You earn just enough to go and experience the world. The journey is the only thing that matters.'

'She's going with her boyfriend next summer,' Claire said once she'd gone downstairs. 'She met him at the Caribbean Club one Thursday.' She was looking at me with her eyebrows raised, like there was a secret code and she was just waiting for me to cotton on.

'He's coloured,' she whispered, leaning in.

'Oh.'

'I've seen a photo. And I'm not talking the guy-from-Hot-Chocolate-black, I'm talking *black* black.'

I didn't know how I was supposed to react, but she was waiting for me to say something.

'Wow.'

'I know. Can you imagine? My parents are gonna go spare.'

I can hear Dad coming upstairs. He takes them two at a time. He knocks on the door but doesn't wait for an answer. I close my eyes and go limp. He stops for a minute. He hesitates.

'Alright, love? You awake?'

I can't help smiling. Mum would've told me to sort myself out and stop being so dramatic. Too late. I've given it away now. I sit up.

'What's all that noise about then?'

I shrug.

He picks the book up off the floor and sits down next to me. He's humming under his breath. He doesn't even know he's doing it.

'Don't you think you'd better get started?'

'I hate woodwork. There's no point.'

He reaches for a pencil on the bedside table. 'What've you got so far?'

I just look at him. He shakes his head.

'Karen Whittaker, you're a bloody pain in the arse.' He looks up to the ceiling for inspiration. 'A bird box or a pencil tidy?'

'Whatever's easier to make.'

'Don't mention this to your mother,' he says and starts to draw.

I sit with my legs crossed, like Claire's sister does when she's trying to meditate. I watch him. He's like a little kid sometimes. He sticks his tongue out when he's concentrating. I could shuffle nearer and put my head on his shoulder and fall asleep. He's a big daft sod. Like Mr Reynolds. But better than Mr Reynolds. I wonder sometimes how he ended up with Mum.

He's gone and I'm tired. There's nothing to do. I can't be bothered to move. Turn off the bedside light and lie down. But it's impossible to sleep with the sound of them coming up through the ceiling. Dad laughing at something on the TV. Both of them downstairs on the sofa drinking milky teas and fighting over the footrest. No room for anyone else. The sketch is far too good. The bird box all straight and perfect on the page. I wonder if Reynolds will let me use the rasps. I can feel the weight of my school skirt, resting over the end of the covers. Voices and music all blurred and distant, like the vicar giving the sermon at church – blah, blah, blah, the sound of it going up and down and up again like a song that nobody knows. And the organist playing everything too slow even when the lyrics tell her otherwise. *Oh, be swift my soul to answer him, be jubilant my feet, our God is marching on.*

Now it's the darkness and the trees. Bird boxes, all wonky with nails bashed in wrong. Simon Williams stripped down to his vest and under-kecks. He hands me a hammer and I take a swing. Before I hit anything a head pops out. I want to scream but no sound comes. It's all trapped in my chest. And the bird is stuck. The hole is too small. Its head is black and white with beady little eyes. They shine in the darkness. It opens its beak and the noise it makes is terrible. Like metal against metal.

I'm awake. I have to turn the light on to shake the panic. The house is quiet. My heart racing. I'm desperate for a pee. I check the clock on the bedside table, listen out for a sound, something that could've woken me up. There's nothing. Just the clock ticking gently. No noise from the yard. Not even next door's cat getting into a fight. There's no drama here but I can't shake the fear. Like someone pressing their hand against your throat. Like the only time Dad ever really lost it, when he pushed me into the hall and held me against the porch door and his hands were so tight on my arm that they left a mark. It was years ago. I haven't thought about it in ages. I was asking for a baby sister. I was asking and asking and Mum just wouldn't listen. She turned away. Back towards the ironing. It was like she couldn't even hear. I pulled on her sleeve. I told her I'd do anything. 'Even a brother,' I said before I'd really thought about it, 'even a little brother.' Dad stood up then. It was so sudden. His face was red. I'd never seen him look like that before. 'Don't talk about this again, do you hear me?' he said, 'it upsets your mother.' I pulled away and ran upstairs and we never spoke about it again.

I try to breathe slowly. Centre myself or whatever it is Claire's sister does. She's probably still up. Imagine it. Thousands of people still awake, right this second, talking their way into the night, dancing in the darkness and falling in love. I need the loo but I don't want to move. Everything is grainy, like the TV when all the programmes are finished for the night. Empty. I can't shake this feeling. I can't make it go away.

There's nothing here and no one to talk to. Everything that really matters in the world is happening right at this second. It's just happening to other people, somewhere else.

7:35 pm

and then you just have to sit and do what
you're told   and watch the   pictures.

There are people on the thingy   and there's water. The
water is drowning the houses. The houses are floating and the
people travel on roofs. I don't know where they're going.
       the carpets are bound to be soaked.
  Policemen and firemen and people on boats. And rain on
the windows. The water rising outside. Coming down from
the heavens and rising from the deep. Coming to wash everything away and start again. I wouldn't mind about the carpet
if the water could take me away. The letters would be soggy
but I could sit on the roof and look for Ned.
Very far, very far, over land and sea.

       I can't get on the roof if the doors don't open.

Here is the church, here is the steeple, open the doors –
              but I don't want the people. I just want him.

       I could give the people a piece of my mind.

20 September 1957

Arthur

It feels like ages since I knocked. Long enough. I put my face up against the glass in the front door. There's no movement inside. No sign of May. All I can smell is the roses. The bushes all staggered and spaced in the border around the lawn. Not the wild kind that used to grow in the hedges by the canal. Nothing like the ones Mum used to pick rosehips off in the autumn. These buggers have been pruned and coddled to within an inch of their life. The branches all stumpy where they've been cut back. More thorns than flowers. I check the bar of chocolate in my pocket. Move it across to the shady side so it doesn't melt. Pull my jacket down, make sure my shirt is tucked in right. Knock again. I risk a postman's special. Loud enough to wake the dead. Or, at the very least, Mrs Pye on Bird Street who's deaf in one ear and drinks so much she doesn't surface till the middle of the afternoon. And then I see her – May – coming to the door. The shape of her warped through the bubbled glass. *Ask and ye shall receive*, Mum used to say whenever we had a bit of good luck, taking the piss in her pretend posh voice, *knock and it shall be opened unto you*.

'What are you doing here?' she says opening the door just enough to hiss at me through the gap. Her eyebrows are all creased up. I want to laugh, or even better – kiss her and give the neighbours something to talk about. I hold up the chocolate like it's an official pass.

'I got sick of waiting for an invitation.'

She lets out a big breath. 'I told you it wasn't the right time, Arthur. I *told* you.'

'Patience isn't my strong suit.'

'Who's that?' The voice comes from the back of the house, 'who's at the door?'

'You've gone and done it now.' She throws her hands up and opens the door wider. I step into the porch. The smell of furniture polish is so strong I have to hold my nose to stop it twitching.

'It's just a friend,' May answers, and her voice is all high and polite, 'I've asked him in for tea.'

There's no reply. Just the sound of the clock ticking in the hall. The staircase winding up. The flowers on the carpet all faded and threadbare. If we were alone I'd get her to give me a tour. Just the thought of it. On our own upstairs.

'Friends now is it?' I lean in. My lips right against her neck.

She turns and puts a hand against my chest to push me back. Snatches the chocolate out of my hand, points to the front room.

'Stop it, Arthur. Just wait in there, will you?'

I listen out for their voices but there's nothing. I'm starting to think this whole thing might be a bit of a cock up. I should've waited for her to be ready, to let me take her for a drive again or catch an early film in town. It's all Jimmy's fault. Him all gung-ho – puffed up and proud of his new little family.

'If you're sure about her don't drag your feet,' he said, 'it's not as if either of you are getting any younger.'

Christine passed him the baby then and Jimmy propped him into the crook of his arm. Little Billy's eyes started to droop, his lips still warm and milky. All three of them the picture of bloody contentment.

I whistle a little tune. Run my finger over the books in the alcove. Shakespeare and Wordsworth, the Book of Common Prayer. A shelf full of cricket almanacs and a photo of her father standing outside the police station and clutching his hat. I lean in to get a better look. The photograph is all creased and ripped at the edges. Like someone screwed it up by mistake and then tried to flatten it back down. There's one of May as a baby too. Pristine. She's laid out on a lacy blanket. Smothered in frills. I try to find her in it, her face as it is now. In the photo she's bald as a coot. But her expression's the same. All deep and serious. I'll tease her about it some time. But not today. I'm on thin enough ice as it is.

There isn't a speck of dust anywhere but it still feels closed and unlived in – a museum piece just for show. Mum could always spot them a mile off, the people with money, the ones who had proper cabinets for the good china and special rooms saved just for visitors. On Blackpool prom they'd be counting out the pennies before going in the shops, the children looking miserable because they had to choose between an ice cream and a go on the donkeys. *No wonder they never run out*, Mum said once, *it's cause they never bloody spend any of it.*

I look out of the big bay window onto the roses and the village green. There are children playing games on the grass, a little boy in shorts running in and out of the trees to try and get away. Then the voices from the hallway. The clink of teacups. I sit down on a perfectly plumped cushion and wait.

'Tea?' May offers, she pulls a table out from a little nest of them by the window and puts the tray on it.

'That'd be lovely.'

Her mouth is tight, the smile forced. I'll be in for it later. Her mother sits down in the armchair in the corner and I have to stop myself from staring. She's nothing like I imagined. Small and pale and absolutely ordinary. She's wearing a paisley dress, a knitted cardigan, stockings that are far too dark for her skin. She looks frail and harmless.

'This is Arthur, Mum. I met him at the post office when he was covering the village round.'

'Nice to meet you, Mrs Matthews.'

'I remember you from the field day,' she says glancing over, 'you visited the tea tent. May never mentioned you'd formed an acquaintance.' She holds out her cup, 'a touch more milk in mine please.'

May's cheeks are all flushed. When she pours her hand is unsteady.

'We don't usually have visitors on Sundays,' her mother says and her eyes settle somewhere on the wall just behind me as if she's talking to my shadow. It makes me wonder about her eyesight. I glance over to May but she's still messing with the tea things. It makes me wonder if there's something wrong with my face.

'We stay at church till one, setting up for the evening service. If you'd come any earlier you'd've had a wasted trip.'

'You'll have to excuse me for dropping in like this Mrs Matthews,' my voice comes out all strangled and clogged, I clear my throat and swallow a couple of times, 'I became a godfather today, you see.'

The tiniest of nods.

'The christening was in town but my friend Jimmy – he's the father – well he grew up out here, on a farm just down the road. There's a get-together afterwards at the old family place. Just a little dinner. I couldn't pass by without saying hello.'

'Catholic?' she says and for a minute I can't think how to answer. I look at May but her face is unreadable.

'Church of England,' I say, although it's not as if I'd really know the difference.

She nods. I've said the right thing. 'Was it a nice service?'

'Lovely,' I take some shortbread from the tray and try to think of a way to keep the conversation going, 'the hymns were... particularly rousing.'

May smiles. Just a little one. It's gone so quickly I can't really be sure. I hold the saucer under my chin to catch the crumbs. Lick the sugar off my lips. The silence is painful.

In the church I couldn't really hear the hymns at all. Not properly. Christine was next to me on the front pew holding little Billy. He wriggled and squawked through the whole service, drowning everything out. Jimmy tried to stroke his cheek but there was nothing doing. When we stood up by the font it was worse. His face was bright red. Little legs kicking at the vicar. I nodded in all the right places. I made promises. There was something about Satan, about helping to cast out the devil. And when the vicar dripped the water on his forehead he was quiet for a blessed minute. He went still, his eyes wide in shock. He took a big breath and closed his eyes and the scream sounded worse than ever after the silence. All the saints in the stained glass windows covering their ears. We laughed when the final prayer was over. The relief. I slapped Jimmy on the back.

'Nothing wrong with his lungs,' the vicar said, filing out behind us down the aisle.

'Your father,' May's mother says out of the blue, 'what did he do in the war?'

I put my cup down on the table. 'Never had a chance to do anything,' I say, 'he died when I was a baby.'

'And was he a redhead too?'

I put my hand up to my hair, 'my mother always liked to call it auburn.'

'There's nothing wrong with red hair,' she says, 'Nothing whatsoever. May's father had hair the colour of a fox's tail. It was so bright they used to say the criminals would see him coming in the dark. Not that that there was ever much call for chasing criminals round here.' She points over to his photo. 'Killed in forty-two. He was a stretcher-bearer. May will have told you?'

I nod but it's all news to me. She's never mentioned that he served in the war. Never talked about him much at all now I come to think of it. I look at her but she won't meet my eye. I always thought the police was a reserved occupation.

'Threw himself across an injured man when a shell came down. Greater love hath no man. Do you know where that's from?'

I take a stab, 'the Bible?'

'John chapter five, verse thirteen. Greater love hath no man but this, that a man lay down his life for his friends. That's the sort of thing that'll get you straight in through the gates no matter what went on before.'

I look at May again. The rash on her neck. Rising up. The music will be starting at Jim's place by now. All the bottles of beer and cider ready for the real head wetting to begin. I want to grab her hand and run to the car. Drive away and sod the consequences. Now her Mum's got going on this topic I have a feeling there won't be any stopping her.

'Here—' she reaches into the pocket of her cardigan and brings out a crumpled envelope. She hands it to me. A letter.

'I keep it on me always. It's from a soldier from the same company who witnessed it all.'

The paper is yellow and starting to go brittle. I open it because I have to, because she's watching me. So many years of being warned off reading other people's post. I can't do any more than scan through. *He was a good man*, it says, *he was a man who always thought of others before himself.* It's all too private.

'He was very brave,' I say because I can't think of anything else. I hand it back to her and wonder how on earth I'm supposed to change the subject. There's no polite way to do it, but time is running out.

'I was wondering, Mrs Matthews, if you could spare May for a couple of hours this evening. She could join the celebrations. It's just a quiet dinner, but my friends would love to meet her.'

May squeezes my hand and I can't tell whether it's excitement or a warning.

'Oh!' her mother says and bends forward clutching her stomach, the cup and saucer starting to slide off her knee. 'Oh!'

May stands up and rushes over. She catches the cup and hands it to me.

'What's the matter?'

She shakes her head at me. 'It's ok, Mum,' she says and rubs her back, 'just breathe as deeply as you can.'

She's groaning and rocking now. The sound is like nothing else.

'What can I do?'

'Nothing,' May says, 'you'd better go.'

'I could help you get her upstairs.'

'Go, Arthur.'

She has that look on her face – as if it's all my fault, as if I should've known better.

In the farmhouse there's nothing but noise and dust. Muddy boots propped in the corner, the smell of mince and onions mixed up with the sour air from outside. I haven't seen half these people in yonks. Not since Mum died and Jimmy started bringing me back for lunch on a Sunday.

'What's up with you?' he says handing me a beer, the baby asleep somehow in all this noise, sprawled against his shoulder.

Old Jim is hovering behind him, already half-pissed. 'He's in love, son that's what,' he gives me a look, as though he's daring me to say otherwise, 'being dangled on a string by a famous local jezebel.' He laughs then and it all gets mixed up with coughing, the rasping, phlegmy sound of it, as though he'll spew his guts up any minute.

'Alright Dad,' Jimmy says, thumping his back, 'it's not that funny. It's not a joke worth dying over. Bugger off over there and get Aunty Betty another drink will you?'

Old Jim stumbles across the room and Jimmy shakes his head at me, 'some things never change.'

'I think I might have buggered everything up – with May, I mean.'

He jiggles the baby up a bit and little Billy raises his head, stretches his wrinkled neck like a blind tortoise, takes a long, shuddering breath and settles back into Jimmy's shoulder.

'No,' he says, 'you're taking it too hard, Arthur. You're right to take matters in hand. Mum says Mrs Matthews is a right piece of work. Always has been. Thought she was Queen of the village until all that funny business—' He looks uncomfortable. Like he's said more than he planned to.

'What do you mean?'

'Ah, nothing. Just village talk that's all. Mum's been in my ear ever since she found out you were sweet on the lass.'

'Well you have to tell me now.'

He shrugs and moves in closer. 'Hasn't May ever mentioned it, her dad and that?'

'What about him?'

'It's before my time, but I've heard things. People round here were surprised they even let him go off to war. He went to pieces. All those years opening village fetes, and dealing with the odd burglary. Then there was that little boy who drowned. Right tragic it was and he just couldn't handle it. They had to bring in the coppers from across town to sort it out.'

'What little boy?'

'Some farm lad from across the way. Funny little thing. Not quite right in the head. Wandered off one day and they found him drowned in a ditch, or was it a slurry pit?' he puts his free hand over Billy's head to shield him, 'doesn't even bear thinking about either way.' He opens his mouth to say something else and then thinks better of it.

'What?'

'Nothing.'

'Go on, Jimmy. You may as well get it all out.'

He shrugs. 'There was talk, that's all. Some people thought there was a bit more to it. The boy's mother was a sweet, pretty little thing. Her husband always half-cooked. A bit of a brute. Kept her in poverty. People didn't see her for months at a time. And the little boy had a look about him, if you see what I mean. They say it was hard to see any of the father in him at all.'

I light a cigarette and stand looking out towards the fields, the line of fells looming dark against the sky. The sun is going down now. The first signs of autumn in the air. I can never get used to the emptiness. I don't quite know what to do with myself. If I could get May out of here and into town things would be better. All the voices from inside. Jimmy's sister going for it, playing *Daisy, Daisy* on the old honky-tonk. I don't feel like singing.

And then she's next to me. May. She's here like a bloody dream.

'Look at you,' I say like an idiot, 'you're all covered in mud.'

Her shoes are caked in it. Her stockings spotted right up to the hemline.

'I got a bit lost in the fields.'

'What are you doing walking around here in the dark?'

'I wanted some fresh air. And it was such a nice evening. I walked and walked and then I was by the crossroads. I thought I may as well pop along and see you.'

I take a breath. I want to pinch myself. Her face is all flushed. The air has done her good. She doesn't seem angry at all.

'Thought you'd be glad to see the back of me after today.' I drop the cig and crush it into the dirt.

She shakes her head and leans against the wall. Her shoulder against my shoulder.

'Is your mum any better?'

'She's asleep anyway.'

'What was it?'

'Gallbladder. She doesn't like doctors. It comes on suddenly sometimes.'

'Right.'

'I'm sorry,' she says and reaches up to touch my face. She pauses for a minute and I just wait. Drinking her in. Then she's kissing me. Really kissing me. Not like the other times, not pushing me away or taking my hand off her back. This time she's pulling me closer, until there's no space between us. Her nose against mine, her body pushing me back against the wall, her hands in my hair. I can't think. My hands are everywhere. I can't get enough. She pulls away and we're both breathing like we've done the hundred-yard dash. The craggy stone digging into the back of my head. I laugh. The surprise of it. In the house they're singing *Lassie from Lancashire* and May starts humming along. She can't hold a tune to save her life.

'You should never have come round in the first place,' she says.

'Well, I'm bloody glad I did now.' I reach for her.

She laughs. 'Arthur,' she says.

'Why don't you come in for a minute and say hello?'

'Look at me, I'm a right state.'

'They won't care.'

'I have to get back. Mum doesn't know I'm here.'

I want to ask her about her dad and the boy but her face is so peaceful right now. I want to ask her to run away with me and never come back but this isn't the time for it. In years to come I don't want the memory to be poisoned by the smell of cow shit.

'Come on, I'll walk you home.'

'Alright.'

We miss the last chorus of the song running round the corner of the house, jumping over the puddles in the farmyard. I help her up, over the gate and into the lane. The hedges are all overgrown, big long branches waving around above us in the dark. She takes my hand and I don't care about her mother or her father. I don't care about a single thing before this moment. Everything else is just history.

9:23 pm

I'll get into bed if you let me give her a message.

      Lights flashing   dry hands

           people are screaming   somewhere.

      What sort of place is this? Don't answer that, I don't want to know. He leadeth me beside the still water. He leadeth me, he leadeth me

      somewhere.

I'll get into bed when I want, when you give me back my buttons and feathers and   leaves. Tell her to listen, tell her to come. Don't do that

      what sort of place, what sort of racket are you running   I only want to tell her I only want to tell her

I used to play in the puddles with Ned and she brought the wrong boy

I remember there was a fair on the Green and I was wearing my dress with the blue buttons and he was running away, so tiny, and his hair was so bright   and Dad shouted. He said he could wear the helmet if he wanted, but Ned didn't stop and there were rides and music and cakes and he was running

very far.   And that was the last time   that
was the last

    I think I remember but nothing is certain.   I wonder if
they ever found him in the water.

1 June 2007

Alex

The man tells us his name is Keith. He says the best way to learn how to build a dry stone wall is to try and repair one. He stands next to the collapsed section, his wellies sinking into the boggy ground. Across the field there's an empty barn, a lone farmhouse nestled in at the foot of the fell. The wall snakes out, neat and rough at the same time, dividing up the grass. The outward stones are covered in patches of bright green moss, spattered white with bird shit. It doesn't look like any man built it. The broken gap is just a spill of stones. It could have been kicked in by a giant.

'Gather round,' he says and we all move forward, circling the broken stretch of wall like student doctors about to observe an operation.

'The first thing is to clear the stones, to sort them into organised piles to be used later.'

I try to remember the diagram in the library book from college, the layers of construction, the order of it. Foundation stones, through stones, coping stones. *The base width of the wall should be twice the width of the top layer.*

He sets us off looking for specific shapes, tells us to place the stones down gently. 'Especially the through stones,' he says,

'if you just lob them on the ground they're sure to crack.
There's no putting them back together after that.'

Everything's a blur of movement. People staking their terr-
itory, squatting down to lift the heaviest boulders as if they're
actors in a health and safety video. A woman in a red gilet and
muddy jeans asks Keith if the stone she's holding is the right
shape to go on the top layer. When he nods she grins like a
little kid, lays it down, good-edge upwards, next to the others
and high-fives her mate. I want to say it's not a competition.
We're not hunting for fossils or playing Tetris. But there is
something satisfying about the rhythm of it all. I stay at the
edge of the group, nearest the break with the standing wall. I
focus on finding the good, solid building stones. Build my pile.
Make sure there's enough space for when we start construction later. The sun is warm on the back of my neck. I wish I'd
remembered the sun cream. Keith wanders up and down the
line nodding and giving advice. Then he stops to take his top
off, as if it's nothing, as if he's just blowing his nose or scratching an itch. He's in great shape for his age, his face and forearms
as dark as conker shells, his wide chest still quite a few shades
behind.

'Remember, these small stones – this rubble – is just as
important', he says, handing out yellow plastic trugs, his voice
booming out so that somewhere over the next rise a sheep
starts bleating. 'It's called hearting for a reason. When we get
round to the re-building this is what we'll use to fill up any
gaps in the middle, to prop up and level the building stones
so that the face of the wall is neat and balanced.'

I'm sweating now, even though it's not that hot. Most of the big stones are gone so I help gather up the heartings in armfuls and transfer them to the nearest bucket. Some of the fragments are crumbling into red clay at the breaks. The dust coming off onto my gloves, staining them pink. I think of that scene in the Ten Commandments when Charlton Heston kneels in front of the burning bush and listens to God give him the order to go and speak to Pharaoh. The way Nan's face changed when it came on in the home, after someone flicked through the channels, as though she remembered it but not watching it with me. He kneels there and the whole cave is glowing red, the special effects so dated. God's booming American voice, and Charlton's expression a bit hammy as the realisation dawns on him. What he's being asked to do. But something about the way the music surges at that moment gives it weight. Stupid really, the things that set you off. I was wiping my eyes when she came over. Sana. But she didn't let on that she'd seen. She watched with us for a minute.

'Moses?' she said.

I nodded.

'Isn't he supposed to have a problem with speech?'

I nodded again, and suddenly Charlton Heston seemed even more ridiculous with his handsome confidence, his face tanned by makeup but still so very white.

'The story about the angel putting hot coals in his mouth when he was a child,' she said, 'do you have that too?'

I racked my brains. 'Don't think so.'

She perched there on the arm of the chair and I watched

her play with the ends of her hair, cut so much shorter than usual, dark against her skin. I watched her face as she watched Moses kneel in front of the burning bush and plead inadequacy. I wanted to ask her what she did about her boyfriend in the end and if she was ok and if she wanted to go for coffee after her shift.

'Do you have the plagues?' I said, to keep the conversation going.

'What?'

She looked at me and I could feel myself starting to go red. 'In the Quran, I mean. The plagues of Egypt?'

'Oh. Yes. The frogs. The river of blood.'

I nodded. Always useless at putting things into words. Especially when it matters. Those lessons in high school, in RE where nobody ever gave a shit and I didn't dare to break the mould. That time when the teacher said some people claimed that the Nile turning to blood might not have been actual blood, but red clay disturbed on the riverbed. And I wondered whether that mattered or not, whether it could still be counted as a kind of miracle. Lorna rolled her eyes and whispered in my ear: *Or maybe it's all just a load of made up shit.*

'I've never seen this film before,' Sana said.

Nan sat up then, like she'd been reactivated. She leaned across to Sana. 'Turns out you've not been missing much.'

We both laughed. And all I wanted at that moment was to be somewhere else. With her.

Someone chucks a stone down onto the grass next to me and it misses my foot by a few centimetres. 'It must be time for a break by now,' they say, 'my thighs are bloody killing me.'

Keith lays a big tarp down on the most even patch of grass he can find and we sit there like children opening our lunch-boxes. I find a space nearest the gate and watch the wind ripple over the flooded dip by the stile.

'You serious about this, then?' Keith says, crouching next to me and taking a bite of his sandwich. A thick slab of cheese between two doorstops of bread.

'Sorry?'

'I mean are you here because you actually want to do this – or did you just fancy a nice day out in the country?' He gestures to the others.

One man is wandering to different parts of the field, hold-ing his phone up and checking for a signal. The other is tipping a compartment full of chocolate balls into a plastic triangle of plain yoghurt.

'I'm doing arboriculture at the college –'

'It's a very different thing, trees.'

'Yeah, but I just like working outside, really. I wanted to try something new. I used to walk here with –'

'Don't get many young people on these things,' he says, obviously not interested in the details of my life, 'always look-ing for new blood. You might just be stronger than you look.'

'Thanks,' I say, but he doesn't want any sort of answer. The woman with the gilet gets up to chase an Asda bag that's been lifted in the wind. Keith strides off towards the stile and hops over it, disappearing into the trees on the other side.

'Probably gone for a piss,' the man with the yoghurt says, 'come to think of it I could do with one myself.'

After lunch we work on clearing the last of the rubble, digging out the foundation stones. I stand up to stretch. A couple of crows fly up and land in the tree at the side of the gate. I can't tell what kind it is from here because the bark is covered with moss. The whole thing half dead, young branches warped and split by the weather. It has a haunted look about it. If it wasn't on private land I could use it to practise remedial pruning. I imagine the feel of the knife, blade flipping out, finding the right nick, the best angle, waiting to see if the tree still leaks sap at the cut. Imagine telling Mum I'm switching from trees to stones. Or maybe it's no worse in her eyes. Still a big waste of academic talent. She can't believe I'll ever make any money. I could do neither or both. Just something that means I can stand in a place like this. Something that makes me feel this ache at the end of the day, that means I can lie down in bed and sleep without dreaming.

Somewhere near here is the wall where we stopped and looked up at the old man sleeping. And the village where she grew up. The place she said she'd take me but never did, the stream where she went quiet and looked like she might have seen a ghost.

The others scrape out the soil to make a clean even trench, a solid base to build on. Keith askes me to carry the excess and use it to fill the damp ruts all over the grass, left there by tractor tyres. It's good to get away from the noise of the group.

Sunday school songs on repeat in my head. *The wise man built his house upon the rock and the rain came tumbling down.*

On the OS map the fells are just collections of orange contour lines. It's hard to imagine the curves of them softened by trees, the bleached grass, the heather, the way they loom over you in twilight or when a storm is heading in. The summit cairns no more than piles of rubble. The weekend hang gliders with their bright colours pulled and pushed by the wind.

My phone vibrates in my pocket and I almost drop the bucket. Most of the time it's easy to forget I even have the thing. I empty the soil, wipe my hands and and flip the phone open. The battery's low. I must have wandered into a rare bit of signal because the thing is buzzing for England. Seven missed calls from Mum and a message from an unknown number. *Alex*, it says, *you need to come now. Sana.* I stare at her name for too long. Wonder how she got hold of my number. Suddenly I'm sure my neck is burnt and I'll be in agony with it all night. I'll need to soak a hand towel in cold water and hold it there to calm the sting. I look back across the field, the gap in the wall so stark now, the sections on either side stepped down so that you can see all the inner workings, see the gaps where the heartings should be. I start to run.

I imagine, over the rise and past the next village, the old man waking up, moving his legs so the fields underneath him crumble and split. Pulling at the trees to free his hair, wrenching them up by their roots. When he breathes it sounds like the wind. He doesn't stop to look where he puts his feet. He kicks a hole, for no good reason, in every wall he can find.

'Sorry, have to go,' I say to Keith, grabbing my bag, patting my pockets to make sure I have the car key.

He shrugs as if it makes no odds to him. 'Gotta do what you gotta do,' he says, and carries on working, checking the trench for stones and lumps, pushing the others to keep scraping out the soil, pointing out to them all the things that only he can see.

11:57 pm

These sheets are so tight and the
        darkness   is here and the water
dripping

don't think these hands will ever   mend on their own.

There are things I have to tell him. They put me here and leave me here and nothing is settled.

And then one day, one magic day he'll come this way and when he comes he'll see to it all. He'll find everything that's lost. Every knee, every tongue, every pair of hands. There'll be nothing left to do. When he comes he'll open his arms and there'll be so much light and green no one will stop us and the water will be gone forever and he'll tell them all, he'll remember, he'll know the greatest thing – the important thing – the thing that's always, always just a bit too far away to reach –

Repeat it so you'll remember. Repeat it or you'll only forget. *The greatest thing you'll ever learn*, the greatest thing, the *greatest* thing is –

Acknowledgements

Thanks to the AHRC for awarding me the funding that allowed me to research and complete this novel. To Graham Mort and Mike Greaney for being such encouraging supervisors and pushing me to experiment. To Jonathan Taylor and George Green for advice that helped me find the best way to bridge the gap between PhD and publishing. To staff and fellow students in the Department of English and Creative Writing at Lancaster University for continual support and advice. To Yvonne Battle-Felton for positivity, inspiration and generally being my unofficial life-coach. To Vicki Howarth and Aasiya Mota for early reading and valuable opinion.

Thanks to Penny Thomas for the most generous rejection I ever received and believing in the novel enough to give it a second chance. To Mick Felton and all at Seren for producing such a beautiful book and pushing me to make it better. To Nemonie Craven for astute feedback and insight – thank you for helping me remove the red herrings and deepen connections.

To my family and friends – thank you for being in my corner. Writing is solitary (even for an introvert) and it's easy to lose hope!

Finally, to Stephan and Anna, for beautiful(and necessary) distractions, and never letting me give up.

About the Author

Naomi Krüger's short stories have been published in various literary journals and her first novel manuscript was highly commended in the Yeovil Literary Prize 2014. She has an MA and PhD from Lancaster University and currently lectures in Literature and Creative Writing at the University of Central Lancashire where she researches representations of cognitive impairment in fiction as well as working on new writing projects. She is also the co-creative director of North West Literary Arts, an organization facilitating events and community projects in Lancashire.

The idea for *May*, and her interest in memory and representations of dementia, followed a visit to a family friend in the early stages of dementia who remembered things about Naomi's own life that she herself had forgotten. Naomi was born in Preston and still lives there with her husband and daughter.